'Hi, Mum!' Allegra bounced across and gave her mother a hug. 'Jade's back!'

'Oh, good,' said Paula, turning round. 'How was school? Oh my . . . Jade! Oh!'

She clamped her hand to her mouth and grabbed the back of the kitchen chair for support.

'What have you done?' she wailed. 'Your lovely hair? Jade, how could you!'

Jade took a deep breath.

'It's my hair and I can do what I like with it.'

What a Week

to Break
Free

Rosie Rushton

PUFFIN BOOKS

For Kate who invented Shiny Vinyl,
and for all the pupils of the
Royal High School, Edinburgh

PUFFIN BOOKS

Published by the Penguin Group
Penguin Books Ltd, 27 Wrights Lane, London W8 5TZ, England
Penguin Putnam Inc., 375 Hudson Street, New York, New York 10014, USA
Penguin Books Australia Ltd, Ringwood, Victoria, Australia
Penguin Books Canada Ltd, 10 Alcorn Avenue, Toronto, Ontario, Canada M4V 3B2
Penguin Books (NZ) Ltd, 182–190 Wairau Road, Auckland 10, New Zealand

Penguin Books Ltd, Registered Offices: Harmondsworth, Middlesex, England

First published 1998
3 5 7 9 10 8 6 4 2

Copyright © Rosie Rushton, 1998
All rights reserved

The moral right of the author has been asserted

Set in Monotype Baskerville
Typeset by Rowland Phototypesetting Limited,
Bury St Edmunds, Suffolk

Made and printed in England by Clays Ltd, St Ives plc

British Library Cataloguing in Publication Data
A CIP catalogue record for this book is
available from the British Library

ISBN 0–140–38762–5

MONDAY

Jade Williams rolled over in bed and opened one eye. And just for a moment, she thought she was back in her attic bedroom in Brighton and that the last six months had been one very long bad dream. For an instant she imagined she could hear her father's cheerful, if somewhat tuneless, singing as he beat Jade into the bathroom, and half expected the door to open and her mum to appear with a mug of tea, teasing her about being the sleepiest teenager in town.

But then her eyes fell on the prone form in the bed next to hers, and she remembered that these days she had to share a room with Allegra, the cousin from hell.

She picked up the silver photograph frame on her bedside table and stared at it.

1

'Oh, why did you have to die?' she said out loud to her smiling parents. 'Why did you have to go and leave me?'

They smiled wordlessly back.

'Oh, please! It's bad enough having pictures of dead people all round the room, without you holding conversations with them!'

Jade turned round. Allegra was propped up in the adjoining bed, leaning on one arm and giving Jade the sort of look normally reserved for lower forms of reptilian life.

'Oh, shut up!' spat Jade, trying hard not to cry, mortified that she had been overheard. 'It's all right for you, your parents are still alive. Mine are –'

'Dead. I know. You keep telling me,' yawned Allegra, running her fingers through her mahogany-brown hair. 'Isn't it time you stopped wallowing in self-pity and got on with life?'

She clamped her hand to her mouth in mock dismay.

'Oh, sorry, Jade, I forgot. You haven't got a life, have you?' she sneered, swinging her long tanned legs out of bed and standing up. 'You just loll around looking pathetic and driving us all demented. My mother says it's time you pulled yourself together.'

'Oh, does she?' yelled Jade, grabbing her bathrobe and heading for the door. 'Well, I don't care what she says. It's not up to her. She's not my mother.'

'A fact', snarled Allegra, picking up her hairbrush and following her, 'for which I imagine she is truly

2

thankful. My parents didn't have to take you in, you know. They only did it because there wasn't anyone else, I heard them say so.'

Jade caught her breath. She knew it. They were all sick of having her around. Joshua, who was sixteen and a total dweeb, had ignored her from the start, but then Joshua ignored most people unless they happened to be fascinated by his collection of stick insects and spiders and other revolting creatures which he kept in glass tanks in his bedroom. Nell, who was seven years old, small, chubby and apparently terrified of practically everything in the universe, had been delighted to have a cousin who would read *The BFG* over and over again. But recently she had refused to speak to her and pushed her away when Jade tried to hug her. David, Paula's husband, would smile at Jade in a vague sort of way, as if trying to recall who she was. And even Paula, who had been nice in the beginning, had changed lately. She used to cook all her favourite dishes, and make sure that no one watched the regional news on television in case they reported a car crash and made Jade cry, but lately she had been snappy and impatient whenever Jade mentioned her parents or the past. Jade was pretty certain that the whole family would like her to disappear.

'At least we have next weekend to look forward to,' said Allegra as if to reinforce her thoughts. 'You don't know how good it's going to be not having you dripping around the place all the time.'

Jade whirled round to face her, her hand on the door handle.

'Not half as good as being miles away from you!' she shouted. 'I wish the school trip was for a month, not just three days. In fact, I wish I could just go to Dorset and never come back!'

'You and me both!' retorted Allegra. 'Now, if you don't mind, I want a shower.'

She pushed Jade to one side and opened the door.

'It's my turn to go first!' shouted Jade.

'Tough!' replied Allegra.

Jade glowered at her.

'That's not fair!' she shouted. 'Why should you always have things your way?'

Allegra turned and gave her a condescending smirk.

'Because', she said snippily, 'I was here first. Remember?'

And with that, she disappeared into the bathroom and slammed the door.

Jade sank down on to her bed and gazed miserably at the photographs. Her mother and father were frozen in time, beaming at her from behind the glass, as if they didn't have a care in the world. Dad wouldn't sing songs in the shower ever again and Mum wouldn't nag her to get a move on. They were dead, killed by a teenage joyrider in a stolen car. And because of that, Jade was living 120 miles away from her gran and all her old friends, feeling as if she would never properly belong anywhere again.

She knew she should be feeling a rush of love, or a sharp stab of sadness, but instead she was overcome by a violent, gut-wrenching anger. Anger with them for dying, for abandoning her to this ready-made family, who were already tired of being kind and were starting to make it quite clear that they wished she wasn't around. And no one was better at doing that than Allegra. Allegra hated her.

'Of course she doesn't hate you, darling!' her aunt, Paula, had exclaimed the previous Saturday when Jade complained that no matter how hard she tried, her fifteen-year-old cousin was determined to make her life a misery. 'She loves having you here, we all do. Although –'

'Although what?' Jade had retorted. 'Although you wish Mum and Dad hadn't made you guardians in their will? Although you wish there was someone else to palm me off on?'

'JADE! For heaven's sake!' Paula had burst out, slamming the bread knife down on the kitchen counter top and clenching her fists.

She had closed her eyes, taken a deep breath and turned to face her niece.

'I'm sorry, sweetheart,' she had said, steadying her voice and giving Jade a hug. 'All I meant was that . . . well, you should try not to dwell on things so much. It's been six months now and it's time you were putting it all behind you. It does make it hard for Allegra, for all of us to –'

'Hard for you?' Jade had stormed, shrugging her

away and choking back tears. 'Oh, and I suppose you think that it has been a real doddle for me, is that it? You think I should just forget about my parents, like you have. Well, you may not care that Dad and Mum are dead, but I do!'

She had seen the shadow pass across her aunt's face and had waited for Paula to protest that of course she cared, that she missed her sister and brother-in-law just as much as Jade. But she hadn't. She had merely taken a deep breath and carried on chopping vegetables.

'It doesn't do you any good to brood, Jade,' she had said. 'There's nothing to be gained from looking back.'

But Jade couldn't help looking back. The awful thing was that already there were odd moments when she would shut her eyes and be unable to picture her father's face. Or to hear the sound of her mother's voice inside her head. She was terrified that one day she might forget completely. Just as Paula appeared to have done.

Jade could remember her mother, Lizzie, saying that she and Paula had been really close as children so it seemed odd that her aunt never wanted to chat about things now. She could have talked to Gran, but Gran had gone to America to stay with her sister after Dad died and although Jade had received postcards, she hadn't a clue when she would be home.

A tear trickled down her cheek.

'Oh, puh-leese, you're not going all pathetic again,

are you?' Allegra, a towel wrapped turban-style round her head, crashed back into the bedroom. 'By the way, there's no hot water left.'

'What?' gasped Jade. 'There has to be – I've got to wash my hair before school. It looks a real mess.'

Allegra gave a sarcastic laugh.

'What's unusual about that?' she jibed. 'You've had that same hairstyle – well, no, sorry, I can't even call it a style – since you were about eight. Even Nell wouldn't be seen dead in baby curls. I think it's going to take a little more than a hair wash to make you look halfway decent.'

'I hate you!' spat Jade.

'The feeling', replied Allegra, 'is entirely mutual.'

7.30 a.m. Behind closed doors

After a ten-minute battle with her hair, in which the score was Hair 5, Jade Nil, she stomped downstairs to breakfast. The sooner she had something to eat, the sooner she could leave for school. While most of her friends hated Monday mornings, Jade was actually relieved to get out of the house. When she was with Holly, Tansy and Cleo, she could forget her problems and even go for a whole day without thinking of her parents. Best of all, she would be with Scott. She had never had a proper boyfriend before and just thinking about him made her toes curl and little shivers dance up and down her spine. This weekend had been worse than most, because Scott had gone to a family wedding in London and it had been sixty-one hours and thirty minutes since she had seen him. But next weekend, she thought with a grin, she would have him for three whole days. Year Nine's trip to the Hoppinghill Activity Centre in Dorset was the highlight of the term and although Mr Boardman, the headmaster, told them that it was intended to build their characters and improve their communication skills, everyone else (especially Holly) saw it as a mega-good opportunity to get in some serious chatting up behind the rocks they were supposed to be climbing.

All these thoughts of Scott and passion cheered her up enormously and she ran along the hall towards the kitchen, eager to swallow a bowl of cereal and get to school early enough to spend time with him before first period. And what's more, she'd ask Paula for some money to get her hair cut. She knew her aunt was dead against it because she'd tried it on once before.

'Darling, your hair is lovely as it is,' she had protested when Jade had mentioned a new style. 'You look so sweet.'

'I don't want to look sweet!' Jade had shouted. 'I want to look grown up. Of course, if it's left to you I won't ever grow up at all!'

'We'll discuss it later,' Paula had said lamely. But she never had. Today, though, she would. Jade would make sure of that.

It was as she passed her uncle's study that she heard raised voices.

'I've really had just about enough of her,' she heard her aunt complain. 'It's all right for you – you don't have to deal with her whining day after day.'

Jade froze.

'Oh, I expect she'll get over it,' she heard David's calm voice reply. 'Although I must admit, she is very babyish. Perhaps we've all been too soft on her.'

Jade heard her aunt sigh.

'She's so different from Allegra,' she said. 'And I'm not getting any younger. If I'd known that it was going to be this hard, I honestly don't think I would have had her.'

Jade clamped her hand to her mouth to stop herself crying. They really didn't want her. It wasn't just her imagination. They thought she was a baby just because she got tearful sometimes. They wished she was like Allegra.

Then her misery gave way to anger. It wasn't her fault she was here. She hadn't asked for her parents to die. She grabbed her jacket off the hook in the hall. If they wanted her out of their way, she'd keep out of their way.

She snatched up her school bag and opened the front door. Breakfast could wait. She wasn't going to watch them pretending to care, when all the time they couldn't wait for her to go.

She'd show them. She didn't need any of them. Friday couldn't come quickly enough.

8 a.m. 6 Kestrel Close, West Green, Dunchchester. Worrying

While Jade was storming through her front door, Cleo Greenway was pushing a piece of toast disconsolately around her plate and hoping for a miracle before Friday. Maybe, she thought, I will come out in spots, or break my ankle, or start throwing up all over the place. It might even be worth eating rancid prawns if it got me out of going to Dorset.

All her friends were ecstatic at the thought of three days of rock climbing and canoeing and abseiling. Cleo would have preferred to spend the weekend in the dentist's chair having root-canal work than face looking a total nerd in front of the whole of Year Nine.

'I don't know what you're worried about,' her elder sister Portia had said the night before, when Cleo had asked her to breathe all over her in the hopes of passing on her sore throat. 'I had a brill time when I went.'

It was, thought Cleo, easy to have a brill time when you were five-foot-ten, slim as a reed and thought hurling yourself off a viaduct on the end of a piece of rope was a great way to spend a Saturday. It wasn't quite so simple when you were five-foot-four, fat, and totally uncoordinated.

'You're not fat,' Holly would protest whenever Cleo bemoaned her flabby thighs. 'You're just well built.'

Cleo didn't want to be well built. She wanted to be

slim with legs up to her armpits and the ability to do the 100-metres hurdles without the need of a life-support system at the finishing line. She was sure that if she went on this wretched activity weekend, she would be the one who capsized her canoe or got stuck halfway up a rock face.

But even more worrying than what would happen during the day, was what might occur at night. What if she had one of her bad dreams? And shouted out? Everyone would hear her. She couldn't go. She would simply have to think of something. Maybe she should start praying now.

'Darling, there you are!' Her mother, Diana, burst into the kitchen, dressed in a crimson kaftan and matching embroidered Chinese slippers, and waving a letter above her head. 'Sweetheart, the most divine news! You'll never guess!'

Cleo grinned despite herself. Her mother was an actress and even when she was out of work, which was rather too much of the time, she managed to make the most mundane event sound as dramatic as the first moon landing.

'Darling, it's just too exciting!' enthused Diana, waving the letter under her nose. 'I've got a screen test!'

Cleo's eyes widened. Now that *was* news. When she was younger, her mother had done two seasons with the Royal Shakespeare Company, but the arrival of three daughters in quick succession had put a stop to that. Then Mum and Dad had split up and

Mum had married Roy and by the time she returned to acting, it seemed everyone had forgotten her. She did get a few small parts; Cleo's friends had been fairly excited a few months before when her mother appeared, sipping a tomato juice, in the Rovers Return on *Coronation Street*, and there had been a high spot when she was in a film with Andie MacDowell for a whole thirteen seconds, playing 'woman at bus stop'. But the big time had passed her by, a fact which Cleo knew upset her mother enormously. A screen test, however, sounded hugely promising.

'That's brilliant, Mum!' she exclaimed, shrugging her arms into her school blazer and glancing at the clock. 'What's it for?'

'Fittinix,' said her mother, dropping her eyes slightly and sipping her coffee.

'Pardon?' asked Cleo.

'You know, angel,' said her mother, 'those new knickers – the ones that flatten your tummy and make your bottom invisible. They want a more mature woman for the TV advertising campaign.'

Cleo's jaw dropped and she stared at her mother.

'You are not telling me', she said in disbelief, 'that you intend to appear on national television in your underwear?'

Diana nodded enthusiastically.

'It's rather flattering, don't you think, to be chosen for one's bottom at the age of forty-four? You know, if the campaign took off, I could end up as Rear of the Year. What fun!'

Cleo cringed. The idea of her mother's bottom being displayed on TV at peak-viewing time was bad enough. That it should feature on the pages of every tabloid newspaper and be giggled over by every kid at West Green Upper was simply too much to contemplate.

'Mum, you can't! What will Roy think? Does he know?' Cleo could hardly imagine that her chauvinistic stepfather would warm to the idea of his wife making an exhibition of herself in public.

'No, he doesn't know yet – he's left for work,' Diana snapped. 'Anyway, what he thinks is irrelevant. I am my own woman. No man tells me how to live my life.'

Cleo sighed. That's what her mum had said when she and Dad had all those rows before they split up three years ago. And lately, her mother and Roy had been arguing a lot. It worried Cleo a great deal, especially since whenever they had a row, Lettie threw up and Portia stormed out of the house, because she said the tension was bad for her karma. While her sisters were throwing wobblies, her mother would get one of her heads and her stepfather would lock himself in the garden shed, muttering, 'If I had known it would be like this, I would never have taken them on.' It was left to Cleo to calm everyone down.

'You're so sensible, darling,' her mother would croon afterwards. Sometimes, Cleo wished she was the one being pacified with chocolate buttons instead of Lettie. Everyone spoiled Lettie. Still, she thought, if Mum gets work, Roy will be pleased and maybe the rows will stop. I would just rather she found something that involved remaining fully clothed.

'The trouble is,' continued Diana, interrupting Cleo's thoughts, 'the screen test is on Saturday – Roy will be at that golf tournament at The Belfry, Portia's going to Stratford with the sixth form and you'll be away in Dorset. I just don't know what I can do with Lettie. I have to leave for London at six in the morning.'

If I offer to look after Lettie, I won't have to go to Dorset, thought Cleo gleefully. I won't have to worry about dangerous sports or nightmares.

'I won't go to Dorset,' she said eagerly. 'I don't much want to anyway.'

'Of course you want to go, darling!' exclaimed her mother.

'No, truly, I –'

'Sweetheart, it's divinely dear of you but I wouldn't dream of stopping you. All your friends will be there. And that nice new boyfriend – Trig, isn't it?'

Cleo nodded. There was that, of course. Three days with Trig would be good. She had to admit she was surprised that Trig wasn't as determined as she was to find a way out. After all, he hated sport and was desperately self-conscious about the huge strawberry birthmark which covered his body from his shoulders to his waist. But when she had suggested that they work out a ruse together to get out of going, he had refused.

'My dad's really chuffed that I'm going,' he said. 'You know what a disappointment I am to him. And there must be something there that I'll be good at.'

Mr Roscoe was the sort of father who thought sons should spend their time kicking balls and leaping over hurdles. Trig was trying hard to please him and failing miserably.

'That reminds me, angel,' said Cleo's mother, 'I must get you a new sleeping bag.'

'Mum, honestly, don't . . .' Cleo began. And stopped. A particularly detailed image of her mother in cling-fit knickers swam before her eyes. If it was a choice between risking life and limb in a sailing dinghy or making it even easier for her mother to make a spectacle of herself, it would be better to risk drowning.

8.45 a.m. A crisis of confidence

By the time Jade reached the school gates, she was convinced that Allegra was right. She looked a nerd. It wasn't easy to look hip and cool in West Green Upper's dire chocolate-brown and gold uniform but the rest of them seemed to manage it. And it wasn't just rebels like Ella Hankinson, with her platform shoes and drastically shortened skirts, who managed to be trendy. Ursula Newley had put blonde streaks in her hair, which made her look about three years older, and Emily Wilkes had got a babe bob and wore lime-green sunspecs on top of her head, even when it rained.

And I look just the same as always, thought Jade in irritation. Wet, wimpish and boring. Something would have to be done. Fast.

Jade had had long curly hair ever since she was little and suddenly she hated it with a passion. She wished she could take some scissors and chop the lot off right now.

'Hey, Jade! Over here!' She turned to see Holly Vine, waving frantically from the other side of the forecourt. Holly was one of her best friends which was pretty amazing considering that she had really fancied Scott Hamill and even thrown a party in the hope that he would fall madly in love with her. Only it had been Jade he had kissed and Jade he had asked out. Luckily, Holly was the sort of person who fell in love with the utmost ease and only last week she had announced that Scott had been a mere adolescent fantasy and that she was about to embark on a Real Relationship with Paul Bennett who went to Bishop Agnew College, the posh independent school in Oak Hill. Whether or not Paul knew about this impending love affair, Jade was not certain, but as he had just moved into the house behind Holly's, there was no way he was going to be able to shake her off.

'Guess what?' began Holly excitedly as soon as Jade got within earshot. 'Shiny Vinyl are coming to The Danger Zone! On Wednesday! Can you believe it?'

She waved a fluorescent-pink flyer in Jade's face. A somewhat smudged photograph of four faces in mid-shriek stared out from the page.

'Don't you think they are just amazing?' urged Holly, flicking her sleek, nutmeg-brown hair over her shoulders. '*Heaven* magazine says they are going to be really big one day. I would kill to see them play.'

I, thought Jade, would kill to know who on earth they are. Not only do I look a dweeb but I can't even sound hip.

'What's that?' Tansy Meadows panted up to them, her school bag bouncing on her skinny hips. Tansy was Jade's second-best friend, and not someone who liked to be left out of the action.

Jade handed her the flyer, hoping fervently that Tansy wouldn't have a clue as to who they were either.

'Wow!' she exclaimed. 'Wicked! What do you reckon, Jade?'

Jade fixed a bright smile on her face.

'They're great,' she said, hoping she sounded convincing.

To her relief, at that moment the bell rang for Registration.

'Did you understand that French homework?' she asked Holly, hoping desperately to change the subject before she got caught out.

'No,' said Holly, as they pushed their way through the double doors into the school building. 'But then languages and me never did get on.'

She sighed.

'I'd give anything to go,' she said.

'To France?' frowned Jade.

17

'No stupid, to see Shiny Vinyl,' retorted Holly.

'Me too,' said Tansy.

'So why don't you?' asked Jade as they reached their classroom.

'Because of that,' said Holly, stabbing a finger at the small print on the bottom of the leaflet.

Jade and Tansy peered over her shoulder.

'Tickets, currently on sale at Discdate music stores, will not be sold to anyone under age of sixteen,' read Tansy. 'Typical! Honestly, how is anyone supposed to get a life around here?'

'Well, at least there's the weekend to look forward to,' said Jade, dumping her bag on the table and unloading her books. 'That will be cool – with the disco on Saturday and everything. I can't wait, can you?'

Holly stared at her.

'Oh, please,' she said. 'You can hardly compare a school trip with a chance to see Shiny Vinyl. I know which I would rather do.'

'Oh, me too,' said Jade hastily. Now Holly thought she was a nerd as well.

'I suppose', said Holly thoughtfully, perching on the edge of the table, 'we could get someone older to buy our tickets and then hope that we could sort of slide in unnoticed.'

Tansy perked up.

'That', she said eagerly, 'is a brilliant idea. Who? What about your brother, Holly?'

Holly raised her eyes heavenwards.

18

'No way,' she said. 'Ever since he got married and had a kid of his own, he's gone all moral and stuffy and keeps saying things like, "Shouldn't you be studying, Holly?" and "What *are* you wearing?" He'd never agree.'

She paused.

'I know,' she said triumphantly. 'Jade, you can ask Allegra. I mean, I know she's not sixteen but she looks it, and anyway, she's got attitude.'

'Tell me about it,' muttered Jade, miffed at yet another reminder of her cousin's attributes. 'Anyway, I'm not asking her any favours – she hates me and besides, she'd just go and tell Paula and then I'd be for it.'

Holly tossed her head.

'For all you know, she might want to come along – then she'd keep quiet! But I suppose if you're too chicken even to try it, we might as well forget the whole thing!'

Jade took a deep breath and put a bright smile on her face.

'No need,' she said as coolly as she could. 'I'll get the tickets.'

'YOU?' gasped Tansy and Holly in unison. 'Don't be silly!'

'Girls!' Mr Grubb roared, slamming his books on his desk. 'Is it within the realms of possibility that you could silence your over-active tongues for more than ten seconds at a time?'

'Sorry, sir,' they chanted.

19

'You'll never get away with it!' hissed Holly from behind her hand.

'Watch me,' said Jade, and noted with great satisfaction the expressions of sheer amazement on the faces of her two friends.

10.15 a.m. In Geography, deeply regretful
How could I have been so dumb? thought Jade, making a half-hearted attempt to draw a diagram of a glacial valley. They're right; I'll never convince anyone that I'm sixteen. I won't mention it again and they'll just forget about it. That's cool.

11.00 a.m. At break. A quick rethink
'Hi, Jade! Is it true?' Scott flopped down on the bench beside her and grinned. Jade's knees turned to jelly.

'Is what true?' she asked. That I love and adore you? she thought. Yes.

'That you're going to be able to get tickets for Shiny Vinyl?'

Jade took a deep breath.

'Ah, well,' she began. 'I'm not –'

Scott beamed at her.

'I'd never have guessed you'd be up for it! That's so cool. Do you reckon you can get one for me?'

He thought she was cool. He hadn't said she had no chance. She loved him so much.

She looked at him from underneath her eyelashes, the way she had seen Allegra flirt with her snooty boyfriend, Hugo.

'No problem,' she said. 'Consider it done.'

12.30 p.m. In the cafeteria, assessing the odds

'Jade reckons she'll be able to get tickets for Shiny Vinyl, no trouble,' Holly was telling Cleo enthusiastically as Jade came up to the table with her lunch tray. 'That's right, isn't it, Jade?'

Jade bit her lip and nodded half-heartedly.

'You're crazy!' gasped Cleo, attacking her tuna and vegetable bake with enthusiasm. 'You'd never get away with it. You don't even look fourteen, never mind sixteen.'

'Oh, thanks,' muttered Jade. She didn't need Cleo to tell her what she already knew.

'No offence, but she's right,' agreed Tansy, peering with some distaste at the contents of her onion bagel. Her mother was very into natural foods, which meant Tansy kept finding obscure bits of plant life in her lunch box. 'You're the least likely of any of us to pull it off.'

That does it, thought Jade, pulling the ring off her can of lemonade. I'm fed up with the way that everyone sees me as a kid and I'm fed up with people telling me what I can't do. I'll get those tickets if it's the last thing I do.

'I can look any age I like if I put my mind to it,' she said airily.

Cleo frowned and shook her head.

'Even if Jade got the tickets, which is unlikely . . .'

21

Jade glowered at her.

'. . . you'd never get past the bouncers on the door. It wouldn't work.'

'It might', said Tansy thoughtfully, 'if we all wear a lot of make-up and dress really cool.'

'What', insisted Cleo, 'if we get caught?'

Jade shrugged.

'All they can do is chuck us out,' she said. 'It's no big deal.'

Cleo looked at her in stunned silence. She had always thought of Jade as being the one person in their set who was most like her – anxious to do the right thing and keep out of trouble.

'It's worth a try,' said Tansy, warming to the idea. 'Go for it, Jade – you get the tickets and we'll make sure we get in. After all, we've nothing to lose.'

'There is just one small problem,' remarked Holly, tipping the remnants of her crisp bag into her hand and licking them up with her tongue. 'Sorting the parents.'

'Oh, sugar,' said Tansy. 'If my mum hears it's over-sixteens only, she's bound to say no.'

Tansy's mum had been a New-Age traveller when she was young and it seemed very unfair to Tansy that she should have decided to start worrying about convention and common sense and early nights just as Tansy got old enough to do without any of them.

'Mine too,' agreed Holly. 'Why is it parents always imagine that you're going to drink or get in with a bad crowd? As if we'd be that stupid.'

Tansy grinned.

'Best keep their blood pressure down and just say we're going to the cinema together, right? After all, The Danger Zone and the Multiscreen are both in the Rainbow Centre. As long as we stick to the same story, we'll be fine. OK, Cleo?'

Cleo swallowed. She had no intention of going. She didn't like crowded places and she wasn't that keen on indie bands either. But there was no way Jade would get the tickets so it would never happen.

'Fine,' she said. 'Just fine.'

Tansy ditched the onion bagel and peeled a satsuma.

'So are us lot going to share a room at the weekend, then?' she enquired, biting into a segment and squirting juice all down her blouse. 'Beetle said we had to sign the list today.'

Mr Grubb was known as Beetle behind his back, on account of his name and shiny black hair.

'I suppose so,' said Holly unenthusiastically. 'Not that I can bear to contemplate three days away,' she added tragically. 'I shall have to leave Paul behind.'

Jade frowned.

'Paul?' she asked.

'This guy Holly's besotted with,' grinned Tansy.

Jade turned to Holly.

'Are you two an item, then?' she asked.

'Well, not exactly,' admitted Holly. 'But he does

23

fancy me, I know he does. He said hello this morning and he had this look in his eye. He'll realize how he feels any day now and if I'm not here . . .'

Her voice trailed off as the horrific enormity of the situation hit her.

'You could always ask him to the Shiny Vinyl gig,' suggested Jade. 'Shall I get an extra ticket?'

Holly's face lit up.

'Would you? Could I? What will I say? Do you think he'd say yes?'

Jade grinned.

'I very much doubt it,' she laughed.

'Why not?' gasped Holly.

'Because', said Jade, 'he probably wouldn't get a word in edgeways.'

3.30 p.m. In the locker room getting cold feet

'Tansy?'

'Mmmm?'

'Will you come with me to get these tickets? I mean, just for the company. I'll do the talking.'

Jade crossed her fingers behind her back and sent up a silent prayer.

Tansy shook her head.

'Sorry. Drama club. Must dash.'

3.35 p.m. Feet getting colder

'Hey, Holly, wait for me!' Jade ran to catch up with her friend.

'Do you fancy coming into town – to get the tickets?' she asked.

Holly quickened her pace.

'I'm in a tearing hurry – I'm planning to accidentally-on-purpose bump into Paul when he gets off the Bishop Agnew bus. Must run.'

3.40 p.m. Feet nearly numb

'But, Cleo, honestly, it would only take half an hour. Please come.'

Cleo grabbed a sheet of music from her locker.

'I can't – I've got choir practice. Why don't you just forget it? It won't work anyway.'

Oh, thanks, thought Jade. Thanks a bundle.

4.05 p.m.

Shiny Vinyl

AT THE DANGER ZONE
WEDNESDAY 8 P.M.

GET YOUR TICKETS HERE FOR THE ULTIMATE GIG!

Jade took a deep breath and surveyed her reflection in the music-store window. She had tied her hair back in a ponytail and piled on loads of Raspberry Shocker lip-gloss which she had bought at the chemist next door.

'Remember,' she told herself severely, pushing open the shop door, 'it's attitude that counts.'

She strode purposefully up to the counter where a

young guy with greasy hair and a blank expression was chewing gum and gyrating half-heartedly to a rock track.

'Six tickets for Shiny Vinyl, please!' demanded Jade, tossing her head and hoping that she looked mega cool.

'Sorry, love,' said the assistant, hardly pausing in mid-chew. 'Sixteen and over only.'

'I am sixteen,' said Jade, pulling herself to full height, and giving him what she hoped was a sultry smile. 'How much are they?'

'Ten pounds each. And I'm the prime minister of England,' drawled the guy. 'Nice try.'

4.15 p.m. Simmering with rage

Of course, I don't have to tell them that the guy thought I was a dweeby kid, thought Jade, stomping up Abbey Street – Dunchester's main shopping area. I'll just say that I didn't have enough cash on me.

But then, she thought, staring in the window of Gear Change and wondering whether a black lace slip dress would make a difference, if I do that, they'll just give me the money and expect me to go back tomorrow. And I'm not going to look any different tomorrow than I do today. Unless I get the new haircut by then.

That was it! That's what she had to do. That way, she'd get the tickets, and everyone would shut up about how babyish she was and start giving her a bit of respect.

There was just the small problem of how much it would cost. Perhaps she could persuade Paula to cough up her allowance earlier, if she really grovelled. She didn't feel like being nice but if it meant getting a new look, she'd just have to grit her teeth and do it.

4.30 p.m.

Holly stood in the telephone booth, wrinkling her nose. It smelt foul, and she was bored with reading and re-reading the instructions on how to make a call. She wished Paul's bus would hurry up. She had it all worked out. When she saw him getting off the bus, she would run out and bump into him. That way he would have to talk to her.

She knew he fancied her. Or at least, she thought he did. Ever since that Sunday afternoon when Tansy had let on to Paul that Holly liked him, he had eyed her with interest. They hadn't actually had much of a conversation yet, but then as everyone knew, when guys really had the hots for someone, they found speech difficult. It was up to Holly to make it easy for him.

To her relief, the Bishop Agnew school bus lurched into view. Holly's heart beat faster. She peered through the glass and saw Paul, long legged and lean, jump from the step. This is it, she thought to herself. Remember what *Heaven* magazine said. Be cool.

She was about to rush out when she noticed that Paul wasn't alone. He was with another Bishop

Agnew guy and they were deep in conversation. Holly's heart sank. He'd never chat her up now – not with his mate listening in. But she'd give it her best shot anyway.

She shoved the door open and burst out, bumping straight into Paul who jettisoned into his mate, pushing him against the wall.

'Sorry!' she gasped, widening her eyes and trying to look alluring. 'Oh, Paul – I didn't realize it was you! I wasn't looking where I was going.'

Paul grinned. 'Clearly,' he said. 'You OK, Steve?'

The other guy rubbed his elbow and nodded.

'Just about,' he said. 'You're the kid that lives at The Cedars, aren't you?'

Holly bristled. Kid, indeed.

'The one that is mad as a hatter, right?'

Who did this guy think he was? This was not the image she was trying to convey.

'Do I know you?' she asked in what she hoped was an ice-cool voice.

Paul laughed.

'This is my twin brother, Stephen,' he said.

Holly was surprised. He didn't look a bit like Paul who was tall and fair with the most remarkable legs. Stephen was shorter, plumper and had a shock of reddish-brown hair that flopped over his face.

'Take no notice of him, he's a loop,' added Paul.

'*I'm* a loop?' Stephen exclaimed. 'If anyone is loopy round here, it's . . . oh, sorry, what's your name?'

'This is Holly,' said Paul.

Holly's spirits rose. He remembered her name. He'd probably been saying it over and over to himself, plucking up courage to talk to her.

'Well,' said Stephen, 'it's Holly that's loopy. She must be, to fancy you!'

He gave his brother a friendly punch. Paul laughed. Holly thought she might as well lie down in the gutter and quietly die.

'Take no notice of him,' said Paul hurriedly. 'I told him how your friend set you up and pretended that you liked me.'

Holly was relieved that he didn't realize it was she who had made Tansy go with her to drool over Paul a couple of weeks before when he was playing tennis in the park.

'I know it was all a joke,' Paul added. 'Just a laugh.'

Holly swallowed. Now what did she do? They didn't tell you about this bit in *Heaven* magazine.

'Sure!' she said with a bright smile. 'Tansy's always doing that kind of thing for a laugh.'

Paul's expression faltered for just a moment.

'So,' Stephen said as they walked towards Holly's house, 'what do you do when you're not swooning over my brother?'

'Give it a rest, Steve!' snapped Paul.

Go for it, Holly told herself.

'Oh, this and that,' she said airily. 'I'm going to the Shiny Vinyl gig on Wednesday, and then we've got this activity weekend and –'

'Shiny Vinyl?' gasped Steve. 'Wicked!'

29

'Activity weekend?' said Paul at precisely the same moment. 'Where?'

'Dorset,' said Holly, stopping outside her front gate.

'Oh . . . that's nice,' said Paul. 'We're going on one this weekend from school as well. Down in Sussex – sailing and orienteering and canoeing and stuff.'

'He's boat mad,' interjected Steve. 'Now, about this Shiny Vinyl gig . . .'

'I don't suppose by any chance you sail?' Paul continued.

'Off and on,' said Holly casually. Her experience amounted to being sick in her uncle's Laser off the Isle of Wight one windy day last summer but he wasn't to know that.

'Great!' exclaimed Paul. 'Maybe –'

'Never mind sailing,' said Steve. 'How come you can get tickets for this gig? I thought it was sixteen-plus only.'

Holly glared at him in irritation. How dare he interrupt?

'I have connections,' she said.

'Can you get some for us?' asked Steve eagerly.

Us? thought Holly joyfully.

'Yes, I should think so,' she said. Jade had better come up with the goods. This was going to be it.

'Count me out,' said Paul.

Holly's face fell. Steve laughed.

'You should know that my brother is the least hip person I know,' he grinned. 'He'd rather be getting soaked to the skin in a force-five wind than listening to the indie sound. Bad luck, kiddo!'

I think, thought Holly, that I might very much like to kill you.

'It doesn't bother me,' she said. 'And actually, my contact has run out of tickets.'

Steve's face fell.

'So I can't help you,' said Holly. 'Bad luck, kiddo!'

4.45 p.m.

Jade stood at the reception desk of Talking Heads feeling very self-conscious. She wasn't used to hairdressing salons – her mum had always trimmed the split ends for her and the only time she had ever been to a hairdresser was when she was a bridesmaid four years ago.

'Can I help you?' The assistant looked up and smiled.

'I'd like an appointment for tomorrow, please,' said Jade.

'Certainly – what would you like done?'

Jade took a deep breath.

'I want it all cut off. Very short.'

The receptionist tapped a few keys on her computer keyboard and yawned.

'Melanie could do it for you at half-past four,' she said.

Brilliant, thought Jade.

'Er, how much will it cost?' she asked.

'Twenty pounds,' said the receptionist.

'*What?* I mean, that's fine. Thanks. See you tomorrow.'

She'd need all her ingenuity to get that much cash out of Paula. But she'd have to do it. Her street cred depended on it.

5.30 p.m. Plan of campaign

As Jade turned the corner into Lime Avenue, she saw Paula standing at the front door, casting anxious glances up and down the street.

'Jade! Where on earth have you been – I've been worried sick!'

'Sorry,' said Jade in what she hoped was a suitably meek voice. 'Netball practice – I forgot to tell you.'

Paula sighed.

'I've had Nell's teacher on the phone demanding to see me because Nell's falling behind with her reading, and Joshua got bitten by one of his spiders and had to go to Casualty, and I can do without worrying myself silly over you!'

Jade was about to interrupt this outpouring with a stern reminder that she was practically fourteen and quite capable of looking after herself when she remembered that she had planned to be charming.

'I'm really sorry,' she said. 'You have had a bad day. Shall I make you a cup of tea?'

6.00 p.m.

Jade was standing at the kitchen sink, putting part

two of her campaign into action by helping Paula to peel potatoes for supper, when Joshua ambled in with his hand in a bandage, and clutching something black and creepy in a jam jar.

He leaned over his mother's left shoulder and dangled it in her face.

'Aaah! Oh, Josh, take it away, whatever it is. It's revolting. Put it in one of your tanks.'

Josh eyed his new beetle with affection.

'I can't,' he said. 'It would eat the others.' He put an arm on his mother's shoulder.

'Could you sub me for a new tank? Please?'

Paula sighed.

'And if I do, that wretched creature will be locked up for eternity?'

Josh grinned and nodded.

'OK. How much?'

6.10 p.m.

Part three of the campaign involved laying the table. Jade had just got to the napkin-folding bit when Allegra crashed in.

'Mum, can I have ten pounds? Please. It's vitally mega urgent.'

Paula heaved a sigh.

'Allegra, you are always asking for money. What is it this time?'

'*The Deep Blue Sea*'s on at the Rep – Terence Rattigan,' she added.

'I do', said Paula, 'know who wrote it.'

'Yes, well, a group of us are going on Wednesday – it's very educational.'

Paula sighed again.

'OK – get my purse.'

6.15 p.m.

'Can I have some money like Legs and Josh?'

Nell stood in the doorway, chubby and scowling.

'Don't be silly, Nell – what do you need money for?'

'Things,' said Nell.

Paula laughed.

'Well, things will have to wait,' she said. 'Now wash your hands for supper.'

Nell hiccuped and burst into tears.

'It's not fair,' she said. 'You're horrible.'

Slamming the kitchen door, she stomped upstairs.

'Silly child,' muttered Paula.

Jade took a deep breath.

'By the way, Paula,' she said as casually as she could manage, 'could you let me have some money to get my hair cut?'

Paula opened the oven door and prodded the cottage pie.

'I'll trim it for you, sweetheart,' she said. 'Much less expensive.'

'No, I mean a proper cut,' said Jade. 'Short.'

The oven door slammed shut and the saucepans on the hob leapt alarmingly.

'Jade, I've told you,' asserted Paula. 'Short hair wouldn't suit you. Believe me.'

'Oh, great,' said Jade. 'You've decided, have you? Never mind what *I* want to do with *my* hair.'

Paula threw her a warning glance.

Jade tried again

'I only need to borrow a bit,' she said.

'No, Jade,' returned Paula. 'If you want a haircut you will have to wait until you can afford it yourself.'

'Oh, I get it!' yelled Jade. 'It's OK for Josh and Allegra to get handouts whenever they want, but I don't count, do I?'

Paula opened her mouth to speak but Jade was in full flood.

'Well, that's fine by me,' she shouted, 'because I'm going to get my hair cut and there's nothing you can do to stop me!'

6.30 p.m. Little worries

Jade was in the bedroom, seething with fury. It wasn't fair; her mum would never have made such a fuss over something simple like a haircut. Mum used to say that part of growing up was learning to express yourself. Well, Paula could carry on all she liked. Jade wasn't going to be told what to do any longer.

The trouble is, she thought, making bold statements is one thing, but finding the money was quite another. She had eleven pounds left in her bedroom drawer, which wasn't nearly enough for the sassy new hair style she wanted.

She was just debating whether to ask Talking

Heads what they could do for eleven pounds, when she heard sobbing from the next room. She dropped the magazine she was looking at and went on to the landing.

'Nell!' she said, pushing open her door and finding the little girl curled up on the bed with tears streaming down her face. 'What's the matter?'

She crouched down beside the bed and took Nell's hand.

Her cousin snatched it away and sat up.

'Nothing,' she said, sniffing. 'I'm not telling. Nothing.'

She sniffed and rubbed her fists across her eyes.

Jade's heart went out to her. She knew what it was like to sit alone in your room feeling miserable. And she was thirteen, not seven.

'You can tell me, Nell. Maybe I can make it better.'

Nell stared at her solemnly, her big brown eyes filling once more with tears. Jade remembered what Paula had said earlier.

'Is it school?' she asked.

'No, I didn't say that, I didn't!' shouted Nell. 'It's not!'

'OK, OK,' said Jade soothingly. 'I just thought maybe you were worried about your reading.'

Nell screwed her face up.

'Reading's stupid!' she shouted. 'School's stupid! You're stupid! Go away!'

Jade sighed and got to her feet.

'I'll get your mum,' she said. She'd know what to do.

'No!' gasped Nell. 'Please, Jade, don't tell my mum. Look, I'm happy now. See?'

She smiled a watery smile.

Jade grinned back.

'OK, I'll believe you,' she said. 'But tell me if I can help, won't you?'

Nell gulped and nodded her head slowly.

Jade closed the door and went thoughtfully back to her bedroom. She wasn't convinced. She knew that sometimes explaining to people what was really wrong was so hard that it was easier to pretend everything was fine.

6.45 p.m. Cousinly confrontation

'Hey – that's my magazine!' Allegra leaned over Jade's shoulder and snatched it from her hand. 'How dare you touch my stuff!'

'Pardon me for breathing!' retorted Jade. 'I was only looking.'

'Well, don't!' snapped Allegra. 'Buy your own if you want one!'

Jade counted to ten, and then to twenty. She still wanted to kill her cousin.

'Now would you please mind getting lost?' asked Allegra. 'I need peace and quiet to learn my part.'

'What part?' asked Jade.

'Saint Joan,' said Allegra proudly. 'I've got the lead in the school play.'

'Saint Joan?' queried Jade. 'Isn't she the one who got burned at the stake?'

Allegra nodded.

'That's nice,' said Jade. 'What a pity your school won't be using real flames.'

7.15 p.m. On the line

They were halfway through supper when the telephone rang.

'I'll get it!' cried Allegra. 'It's bound to be for me.'

She grabbed the receiver.

'Dunchester eight-double-one-one-two-three. Oh. Yes, she is. Hang on.'

She turned to Jade.

'It's for you,' she said sullenly. 'Holly someone.'

Jade jumped up.

'Jade, did you get them?' Holly shouted so loudly down the phone that Jade was sure that everyone would hear.

'No,' she said.

'I *knew* you wouldn't! You should have asked Allegra!'

'Ssshh!' hissed Jade, looking hastily over her shoulder. 'Anyway, I can get . . . do it, but you have to give me the money.'

'Oh . . . sorry,' said Holly. 'How much?'

Jade was conscious that both Allegra and Nell were staring at her.

'Ten pounds.'

'*What?*' Holly gasped.

'Look, we're eating. I'll call you back.'

She went back to the table and smiled.

'Was you being horrible to her?' demanded Nell, pushing a chip round and round on her plate.

'Not was you, were you,' corrected Paula instinctively. 'Of course she wasn't. Don't be so silly, Nell. Eat your supper.'

Allegra was eyeing Jade with suspicion.

'What do you want ten pounds for?' she demanded.

Jade thought fast.

'Cinema,' she said. 'We're going on Wednesday. I'm in charge of getting the tickets.'

Paula put her knife and fork down with a clatter.

'Oh no,' she said firmly. 'Not on a school night. No way.'

Jade glared at her.

'That's not fair!' she said. 'All my friends are allowed to.'

'Well, I'm not responsible for your friends, but I am in charge of you and the answer is no!'

Jade thumped her fist on the table, sending peas spinning over the tablecloth.

'I don't believe you! You said Allegra could go out this Wednesday – I heard you!'

'Allegra is a year older than you and besides, she's going to the theatre. It's different.'

Jade pushed back her chair and leapt to her feet.

'Oh, well, it would be, wouldn't it?' she stormed. 'You make quite sure everything's different for your kids. I'm just the hanger-on, aren't I? You don't –'

'JADE! David, say something.'

David glaced up from the evening paper he had been reading.

'Apologize to your aunt, Jade,' he said mildly and returned to the financial pages.

'What for? Wanting a life? I'd have thought you'd be pleased I was going out. After all, you don't like me being here, do you?'

Paula was opening her mouth to reply when the front door bell rang.

'I'll get it – then you can all sit and talk about me behind my back!'

Jade stormed out of the kitchen, slamming the door behind her. I mustn't cry, she told herself firmly. I won't give them the satisfaction.

She opened the front door to find a large woman in a wax jacket holding an even larger dog on a lead.

'Oh, jolly good show! You're in,' she said. 'Is there a Miss Williams at this house?'

Jade nodded in surprise.

'Me,' she said.

'Oh, spot on,' she boomed. 'This letter was popped through my door today – it's addressed to thirty-five, you see, not fifty-three.'

She handed Jade a blue and red airmail envelope.

'It's from Gran!' said Jade, without thinking. 'She's always getting things wrong! Oh, sorry – thank you. Thank you ever so much.'

'No probs,' said the woman enthusiastically. 'Get

vague myself sometimes. Anno domini, you know. Come along, Lucretia, walkies!' And with that she bounded off down the path, turning to give Jade a cheery wave.

Jade sat on the bottom of the stairs and ripped open the letter. A twenty-pound note fell out. She picked it up and hugged it to her chest.

Brilliant! she thought. It's an omen. I'm meant to have my hair cut. Now there is nothing Paula can do to stop me.

The thought of getting one up on her aunt was as rewarding as the idea of a new look.

She sat at the bottom of the stairs and attempted to decipher her grandmother's flamboyant handwriting.

> *113 Heath Place,*
> *Westmont,*
> *Illinois,*
> *USA*
>
> *Darling Jade,*
> *By the time you get this letter I shall be home! I've had a marvellous time here with Alice but I must admit I'm ready to get back to normal and more than ready to see my darling granddaughter again. I'm sure you are terribly grown up by now. We've so much to talk about – so when shall it be?*

'Jade! Come and finish your supper.'

Paula, looking flushed, stuck her head round the kitchen door.

'And who was at the door?'

Jade ambled back along the hall, still reading her letter.

'A woman from number thirty-five,' she said. 'She delivered this. It's from Gran.'

Paula began scraping leftovers into the bin and gestured to Jade to finish her cottage pie.

Jade went on reading.

You can help me sort through some of your parents'
pictures – I am sure there are things you would like to have.
I'll be back in Brighton on Friday next – give me a
ring, darling. I can't wait to hear your voice.
Loads of love,
Gran

'She says she's got stuff of Mum and Dad's that I can have. Can I go soon? How about the weekend after next?' Jade begged.

Paula hurled dinner plates into the sink and turned on the tap.

'I can't just drop everything and go tearing down to Sussex,' she said shortly. 'Besides, Allegra has rehearsals on Saturdays.'

Jade glared at her.

'So? You don't have to take me. I can catch a train, you know. I'm not totally incapable.'

'No?' muttered Allegra. 'You had me fooled.'

David threw her a warning glance.

Jade ignored her.

'So can I? Saturday week?'

'No!'

Paula wheeled round to face her. David redirected his warning glance at his wife.

'What do you mean, no?' exploded Jade. 'It's my life, I'll do what I like!'

'I don't mean that you can't go at all, but not yet!' shouted Paula. 'It's too soon. It's –'

'Too soon!' yelled Jade. 'I haven't seen her for six months. I need to see her.'

Paula took a deep breath.

'So, we'll invite her up here,' she said, trying to keep her voice level. 'For a weekend. That would be nice, wouldn't it?'

Jade shook her head vigorously.

'No, it wouldn't! I want to go to Brighton. I want to see Tanya and all my other friends, and my old house and . . . I just want to go back home!'

A shadow passed over Paula's face.

'This is your home,' she said.

'No it isn't!' Jade cried, choking back tears. 'This is where I live. But it isn't home. And it never will be! Brighton is home and I want to go back there!'

And with that she rushed out of the kitchen, up the stairs and into her room. Flinging herself on the bed, she grabbed the photograph of her parents.

'I want to go back!' she shouted at them. 'I hate it here! It's all your fault – why did you have to die? Why? Why? WHY?'

And hurling the picture to the floor, she buried her

face in the pillow and began to cry as if she would never stop.

7.30 p.m.
'Hi, Cleo? Holly. I've spoken to Jade. She didn't get the tickets.'

Thank heavens for that, thought Cleo.

'But don't worry, it's only because we didn't give her any money. She needs ten pounds from each of us. I've told Tansy.'

Cleo swallowed. She didn't want to part with that much money for something she wasn't even keen to go to. But if she said that, she'd sound wet.

'OK,' she said. 'I'll bring it to school tomorrow.'

It would be all right. Jade would never manage to get the tickets. She'd get her money back. No problem.

TUESDAY

'Tansy! Andy's here!'

Tansy was peering in the dressing-table mirror, wishing she had hair that would lie down and behave itself, when her mother called up the stairs.

She grabbed her school bag and opened her door.

'She'll be thrilled that you've called for her,' she heard her mother say as she pounded downstairs.

Tansy cringed. Didn't her mum realize that it was totally uncool to let a guy know that you were even mildly chuffed by his presence? Not that her mother had a clue when it came to men. It had been ages before she worked out who Tansy's own father was, and all the time Tansy was growing up, she had had a series of extraordinarily unsuitable boyfriends.

'So are you two looking forward to your weekend

45

away?' enthused Clarity, beaming at Andy who was standing in the hallway with a broad grin on his face and glasses halfway down his nose. 'Give you a chance to get to know one another better and –'

'MUM!' hissed Tansy. Honestly, she was such a liability. 'We're going. See you at four-thirty.'

She gave her mother a quick kiss, and steered Andy firmly through the front door before Clarity could utter one more embarrassing syllable.

'Guess what!' cried Andy, the instant the front door closed behind them. 'I've had a postcard from Mum – and this time she's actually written lots.'

Tansy beamed at him.

'Brilliant!' she said. 'Where is she?'

Andy's mum had disappeared months before; just walked out one day and never come back. She sent Andy a postcard every few weeks from a different place so the police weren't worried about finding her.

'They say an adult has the right to go off if they want to,' he had told Tansy miserably one day. 'She's not a missing person because she sends us cards. But all she writes is "Love you lots, Mum".'

Tansy thought it was an odd kind of love, just leaving Andy and his little brother, Ricky, like that. Usually when Andy got a postcard he was pretty quiet for a couple of days but now he seemed really excited.

'Listen,' he said excitedly, pushing his glasses up the bridge of his nose and peering at the card.

> Dear Andy,
> I'm thinking of you a lot this week because I know you will be going on a school trip. Have a lovely time. I do miss you, you must believe me. One day I will tell you everything and then maybe you will understand and forgive me.
>   I am writing this sitting by the sea watching the seagulls fighting over bread.
>   I've sent Ricky a Thomas the Tank Engine card – look after him for me.
>   Much love, Mum

'Isn't that brilliant?' he urged.

Tansy swallowed.

'Well, yes,' she replied hesitantly. 'But does she give an address?'

'No, but the postmark says Brighton and Hove,' he said eagerly. 'But that's not the point. Don't you see – she said one day she'll tell me everything. That means she will be coming back.'

Tansy squeezed his hand.

'That's great, Andy.'

'And she knows about the school trip,' he gabbled excitedly. 'Which means someone is telling her all our news – and that someone knows where she is! If only I could find out who it was!'

Tansy felt so sorry for him. It had been bad enough for her to accept the fact that she would never know her real father, but she couldn't imagine what it must be like to have the person you loved most in the world walk out on you.

Andy slipped the card carefully into his jacket pocket.

'I just get the feeling she'll be home really soon.'

Tansy prayed that his hopes for his mum wouldn't be dashed like her own for her unknown dad.

8.10 a.m. 5 Kestrel Close.
Calming troubled waters

While Tansy and Andy were discussing absent parents, Cleo was hovering in the hallway, fiddling with her blonde hair and trying to put off going to school. Behind the closed kitchen door, her mum and step-father were having a row. Another row. And there was no way Cleo was going to leave her mum while Roy was in one of his angry moods.

'I do think I'm in with a good chance for this knicker advert work,' Diana was saying with a pleading tone in her voice. 'And it would pay quite well, you know.'

'Quite well!' thundered Roy. 'It had better pay damn well, the way you spend money! If I had known how you and your confounded kids were going to drain me of cash, I would never have –'

'Never have married me, is that it?' shouted Diana with a catch in her voice. 'I didn't plan to be out of work! You know how many auditions I've been to.'

'Oh yes,' sneered Roy. 'And when you don't get a

job you console yourself by dashing to the shops and spending more money. I can't carry this family single-handedly, and what's more, I don't intend to go on doing it.'

Cleo winced. What did he mean? Was he going to walk out, just like Dad had? If Roy went too, Mum would be in pieces all over again. Roy was horrid when he was in a bad mood but he was OK the rest of the time and she couldn't bear to think of Mum being as upset as she had been after Dad had left.

'You don't have to,' said Diana hastily. 'Max sends money for the girls each month.'

Cleo heard the sound of a fist thumping the kitchen table.

'Oh, yes – a pittance compared with what it costs to clothe them and pay for Lettie's riding lessons, and now there's this activity camp or whatever for Cleo and –'

That did it. Cleo pushed opened the kitchen door.

'Don't keep shouting at Mum!' she cried. 'I won't go on the weekend. If it'll save money, I can cancel.'

Roy turned round and a guilty smile crept across his rugged features.

'I didn't know you were there,' he said. 'It's OK – you go. Saving that amount would be like trying to stop a tidal wave with a teacup. I must get going.'

He paused to pick up his briefcase and newspaper.

'Someone around here has to earn some money,' he stressed, throwing a stern glance at Diana. He left without kissing either of them.

'Are you all right?' whispered Cleo to her mum. 'Let me cancel the weekend and stay home with you.'

Diana's laugh was brittle.

'No way, angel,' she said. 'It will do you good to get away.'

No it won't, thought Cleo.

'But Mum –'

'Darling, I'm fine. Absolutely fine,' insisted her mother.

Cleo wished she believed her.

8.20 a.m. The Cedars. Boy watching

Holly was hanging out of her bedroom window and quietly drooling. From there, she could see into the kitchen window of the house that had been built on what was once her family's vegetable garden – Paul's house. And she could actually see Paul, leaning against the work surface, mug in hand, talking to his mum.

He was divine. He had a body to die for. And he was hers. Well, not quite hers yet, but it was only a matter of time.

As she watched, Paul turned to put his mug in the sink and glanced up. His eye caught hers. Her mouth went dry and, as she lifted her arm to wave to him, he smiled. Her stomach lurched.

He fancied her. She could see it in his eyes. Please God, she prayed, could you make something happen to bring us together? Soon. Very soon. Amen.

8.35 a.m. Love hurts

It was as Jade turned the corner of Lime Avenue that she saw Scott ambling ahead of her along Dulverton Road. She frowned. He usually waited for her outside his house so that they could walk together.

She broke into a run.

'Scott!' she called. 'Wait for me!'

He paused and turned.

'Hi!' she said breathlessly as she drew alongside him and linked her arm through his.

'Hello,' he said somewhat flatly and gently shifted his arm out of way. 'Did you get the tickets?'

Jade frowned.

'No, I need the cash,' she said. 'Ten pounds.'

Scott's eyes widened.

'Oh well, count me out, then,' he said reluctantly. 'There's no way I can spend that amount. I'm skint!'

'But you have to come!' exclaimed Jade. 'Ten pounds isn't that much.'

'Well, it is to me!' snapped Scott. 'Fitz is ill again.'

Jade bit her lip. Fitz was Scott's dog and he adored him with a passion.

'He's never been right since he got stuck on that building site,' Scott said. 'He's losing weight and he's not nearly as bouncy as he used to be. I'm taking him to the vet but my mum says I have to help pay.'

Jade said nothing. If Scott didn't come to the concert, there wasn't much point in going.

'So,' said Scott, changing the subject as the bus pulled up, 'how's things with you?'

'Dire,' she said. 'My gran's back from America and wants me to go and visit.'

'What's dire about that?' he asked.

'Paula won't let me,' she said. 'Can you believe that? She's so selfish – she doesn't want me to see my old friends or anything.'

'Why?' asked Scott, puzzled.

'How should I know?' said Jade. 'Probably because she hates me!'

Scott sighed.

'Don't start all that again,' he said wearily. 'It's pretty obvious she doesn't hate you. You don't ask people to live with you if you hate them.'

'She didn't have any choice!' retorted Jade. 'It was in Mum and Dad's will.'

Scott kicked at a stray pebble on the pavement.

'She could still have said no,' he remarked.

'Whose side are you on anyway?' asked Jade snappily.

'No one's!' returned Scott. 'I'm just getting a bit tired of you going on and on about how hard done by you are. It's getting very boring.'

Jade's heart missed a beat.

'Don't you like me any more?' she whispered.

Scott paused. Rather too long for Jade's liking.

'Yes, of course I do,' he said. 'I'm sorry. I'd just like it if you were a bit more . . . well, cheerful.'

Jade took a deep breath. Scott wanted her cheerful. OK, OK.

'So what about this weekend, then?' she said

brightly. 'Three whole days together. It'll be great, won't it?'

Scott sighed.

'Mmm,' he said.

Jade felt he could have sounded a little more enthusiastic. He was supposed to be in love with her. It must be the worry about Fitz. She'd just have to find ways to take his mind off his dog.

9.00 a.m. West Green Upper School. Change of plan

'What's with this special assembly?' muttered Tansy to Cleo as they filed into the hall.

Cleo shrugged.

'Probably one of Mr Boardman's little pep talks about SATs and keeping noses to the grindstone and making something of ourselves,' she grinned. 'He has to have his little fix of being headmasterly now and again.'

Mr Boardman was waiting for them on the platform.

'I have', he said, 'some unfortunate news.'

A governor's died, thought Holly, eyeing her fingernails and thinking that she really should paint them ready for when she caressed Paul's hair.

Someone's daubed graffiti on the games pavilion, thought Tansy, staring at the way Andy's hair curled into the nape of his neck.

You have unfortunate news, thought Jade sullenly. My whole life's unfortunate right now.

'There has been a serious fire at the Hoppinghill Centre. As a result, I am afraid that the Year Nine activity weekend cannot be held there.'

A gasp went up from the assembled pupils, followed by an outbreak of anguished chattering.

'Oh no!' chorused Tansy, Jade and Holly.

Oh whoopee! thought Cleo, and tried to look sorrowful in front of her friends.

'However,' continued Mr Boardman, holding up a hand for silence, 'all is not lost.'

An expectant hush fell across the room.

'Bishop Agnew College have arranged a similar weekend for their Year Ten pupils at another centre. Luckily for us, their group is quite small and there is space available.'

A murmur rippled between the pupils.

'Provided I get your parents' consent, we shall be joining Bishop Agnew at the Downsview Centre in Sussex!'

'Bishop Agnew!' gasped Holly. 'That's Paul's school! I'm going away with Paul!' Thank you, God, thank you, she added silently in her head.

'Isn't Brighton in Sussex?' Andy whispered to Tansy.

Mr Boardman held up his hand again.

'There will be a wide range of activities on offer and I am sure you will all have a marvellous time. Any questions?'

Jade put up her hand.

'Whereabouts in Sussex is it, sir?' she asked.

'How silly of me not to mention it,' he said. 'The centre is at Poynfield. Just outside Brighton, right by the sea.'

He was gratified to see how delighted at least three of his pupils appeared to be.

11.30 a.m. In the lab but not in the interests of science

Jade wasn't concentrating on the properties of hydrochloric acid. All she could think about was that by Friday night she would be just a few miles from her old home. She would have the chance to phone Gran and tell her how hateful Paula was being. Gran would get it all sorted. She was so excited she could burst.

'Jade!' Tansy called to her as she walked from the Art block to lunch. 'Here's my money for the Shiny Vinyl ticket. Andy's not coming – he has to look after Ricky while his dad works late – and I've told Mum we're going to the cinema so don't let on, will you?'

Jade's excitement evaporated a little. She still had to get these tickets or look a nerd in front of everyone. It seemed daft to be going to all this trouble for a concert she wasn't interested in, but she couldn't get out of it now.

'You will get them, won't you?' queried Tansy.

'Of course,' she said casually. 'Leave it to me.'

4.00 p.m. Preparing to be beautiful

Jade hadn't expected it to be this nerve-racking.

Looking at her reflection in the salon mirror, she wondered whether she dared to go ahead with it. She fingered her long curly hair. When she was little, her dad used to call her Goldilocks and tell her that he never wanted her to cut it off.

But Dad wasn't here and she had to make a fresh start. Wasn't that what everyone was telling her?

'Hi, I'm Melanie,' said a young assistant, holding out a black gown. 'What can I do for you?'

'I want it all cut off,' said Jade in a rush. 'Like this.'

She thrust the picture she had surreptitiously torn from Allegra's magazine at the girl.

'Wow! What a change!' said Melanie, running her fingers through Jade's hair. 'You are quite sure?'

'Yes,' said Jade emphatically. 'Absolutely certain.'

'You don't want the colour change, do you?' asked Melanie, eyeing the picture.

Jade hesitated.

'I suppose you are a bit young . . .' murmured the hairdresser.

'I'll have it,' said Jade.

5.30 p.m. The end result

Don't cry, Jade told herself firmly. Seeing the heap of caramel-blonde curls lying on the floor, and observing this copper-headed stranger with a shaggy five-centimetre crop staring at her from the mirror, she wondered whether she had made the most awful mistake. It didn't look nearly as good on her as it did on the model in the photograph. And she didn't feel full of confidence, as she had thought she would. She felt exposed and vulnerable as if she wasn't quite sure who she was. It was so . . . different.

'Stunning!' drooled Melanie, holding up a mirror to show Jade the back.

'It's a bit . . . spiky,' said Jade.

Melanie looked affronted.

'That's the essence of the look,' she retorted. 'Get some giant earrings on and a bit of make-up and your friends won't know you!'

I suppose it does look quite cool, thought Jade uncertainly. But still . . .

'How old does it make me look?' she asked shyly.

'Oh, sixteen at the very least,' said Melanie, unplugging the hot brush.

Maybe, thought Jade, it's not so bad. In fact, I might quite get to like it. Mightn't I?

5.45 p.m. Success at last

Discdate music store was packed with people by the time Jade got there. She had gone heavy on the lip-gloss and eyeliner, and just hoped that the school uniform wouldn't detract from her new-found sophistication.

She took a deep breath and strode up to the counter.

'Four tickets for Shiny Vinyl tomorrow, please,' she said, pulling four ten-pound notes from her purse.

'Sure,' said the guy. 'Forty pounds, please. Doors open at seventy-thirty p.m. No refunds.'

He handed her the tickets.

'Enjoy!' he said.

I did it, thought Jade in amazement. I really did it. I'm not a kid any more. I've got attitude. It was worth the haircut.

She ran her hand over the short layers. It would grow, of course. And the colour wasn't permanent. It was no big deal.

It was while she was on the bus travelling home that it occurred to her that she still had to face the one person who would undoubtedly think it was a *very* big deal.

6.00 p.m. Hair-raising reactions

When Jade arrived home, Paula was out. She sped upstairs and crashed into the bedroom, anxious to have another look at her hair before facing the inevitable argument.

To her dismay, Allegra was sitting on the end of the bed, varnishing her toenails.

'Don't come near me,' she began, turning to face Jade. 'You'll only smudge my . . . Jade! Your hair!'

Jade grinned.

'What have you done to it? It's . . . it's . . . so short!' Allegra gasped. 'And the colour – it's red!'

'Burnished Bronze, actually,' retorted Jade.

Allegra stared at Jade for a long moment without speaking.

'My mother will kill you,' she said eventually.

Jade shrugged.

'Tough,' she said. 'It's done now.'

'It doesn't suit you,' said Allegra snidely. 'And it's badly cut at the back.'

'Oh, and what would you know?' retorted Jade. 'That's the essence of the look. It's done for impact.'

Downstairs a door slammed.

'Mum's back!' smirked Allegra. 'Now you'll find out all about impact. Come on – this I have to see!'

Paula was in the kitchen, unloading supermarket bags.

'Hi, Mum!' Allegra bounced across and gave her mother a hug. 'Jade's back!'

'Oh, good,' said Paula, turning round. 'How was school? Oh my . . . Jade! Oh!'

She clamped her hand to her mouth and grabbed the back of the kitchen chair for support.

'What have you done?' she wailed. 'Your lovely hair? Jade, how could you!'

Jade took a deep breath.

'It's my hair and I can do what I like with it.'

Paula was close to tears.

'It's awful! And that hideous colour – it's so brash, so tacky.'

Paula slumped into the chair.

'How could you be so thoughtless, so stupid? How do you think your mother would feel?'

Allegra gasped. Jade gulped. She felt really guilty. Her mum would have hated it. She knew that. But then she knew she couldn't stay looking the same for ever either.

'Mum, that's not fair.' Jade looked in astonishment as Allegra spoke. 'Jade can't go through life doing what you assume Auntie Lizzie would have wanted. Auntie Lizzie's dead, Jade's alive.'

She paused, obviously stunned at her outpouring.

'Not that I'm saying that's a good thing,' she added hastily, reverting to her normal sarcasm. 'But it's not the end of the world. The hair will grow and that awful red will wash out. It's no big deal.'

Paula sniffed and wiped her eyes on a tea towel. Jade was speechless. If anyone had told her that Allegra would ever stand up for her, she would have told them they were mad.

But there was something else. Paula had mentioned Mum. And that hadn't happened in weeks. Maybe it was only by making her aunt cross that she was ever going to get her to talk. It was a thought.

'I had been considering allowing you to go to the cinema tomorrow,' said her aunt. 'But you can forget it. You're grounded.'

Jade stared at her.

'You can't!' she breathed. 'You can't do that to me!'

Paula pursed her lips.

'Oh, can't I?' she said. 'Just watch me.'

'Thanks for standing up for me,' muttered Jade to Allegra as they went upstairs.

60

Allegra shrugged.

'Well, at least you weren't being your normal wimp-like self,' she said. 'That was a pretty brave thing to do – even if you do look like an angry radish.'

Jade glared at her.

'I can't believe she grounded me,' she moaned. 'I simply have to go out tomorrow night. I have to.'

Allegra eyed her sharply.

'Why? What's so special about tomorrow?'

Jade paused. Could she confide in Allegra?

'Playing out with your little friends, are you?'

No, she couldn't.

'Oh, go boil your head,' Jade said.

Jade was coming out of the bathroom when she bumped into Nell on the landing.

Nell stared at her wide-eyed.

'Who did that to you?' she asked, her eyes filling with tears.

Jade looked at her in bewilderment.

'What are you on about, Nell?' she said. 'The hairdresser did it. I wanted it short. Don't you like it?'

Nell shook her head furiously and stomped downstairs.

Oh, terrific, thought Jade. So much for new looks. She began to wonder how long it would take to grow her hair back.

WEDNESDAY

8 a.m. The Cedars. A question of fashion

'Mum, I need some clothes. Mega urgently.' Holly stood in the doorway of the kitchen, knowing that when requests for cash were forthcoming, her mother was prone to look for a speedy escape.

Angela Vine looked up from the list of figures over which she was tutting with ever-increasing impatience.

'Oh, darling, don't be silly!' she admonished. 'You have a wardrobe full of clothes. What on earth do you need more for?'

It never ceased to amaze Holly that a woman who could organize the fund-raising for Women's Centres and keep the accounts for at least three charities had such a poor grasp of life's essentials.

'Because', said Holly patiently, 'of this weekend. I need a new sweater, trainers, some hipsters, and I've seen this amazing tie-dye T-shirt, and –'

Angela put down her pen in exasperation and pushed back her chair.

'Holly, this is an activity weekend, not a session on the catwalks of Paris,' she said. 'You need trainers, I agree, but apart from that you can take what you've got.'

'Mum!' cried Holly. 'Get real! There's a disco on the Saturday night and anyway, I can't wear things my friends have already seen.'

Not with Paul there, I can't, she thought. I need to look sexy yet mysterious, trendy yet classic . . .

'OK,' compromised her mother. 'The shirt and the trainers. That is it.'

'You are', said Holly, 'a very hard woman.'

8.10 a.m. Perfect timing

Holly was hovering near the front door, checking her wristwatch to ensure that she left the house at precisely the right moment to bump into Paul, when the bell rang.

She opened to door to find him standing on the step.

'Hi there,' he said. 'Listen, I was wondering. There's this film on tonight at MGM – *Spinnaker* – all about these guys who restore this tall ship and sail round the world and I thought, as you're keen on sailing . . .'

I am? thought Holly. Oh, yes. I am supposed to be, aren't I?

'. . . you might like to come. With me.'

Holly stood stock still, savouring the shiver that cascaded from her head to her toes. He'd done it. He'd acknowledged that he adored her. He'd asked her out.

'I'd love to,' she said.

'You would?' said Paul. 'Great. I was afraid you might still be going to that gig thing at The Danger Zone. My brother's really miffed that you couldn't get him a ticket.'

Sugar! thought Holly. I'd forgotten all about it. Suddenly the appeal of Shiny Vinyl paled into insignificance when compared to the allure of three hours with Paul. But she'd promised the others.

She opened her mouth. And closed it.

Jade wouldn't have managed to get the tickets. Not in a million years. And if she said no to Paul, only to find that Jade had messed up, she'd never forgive herself.

'No,' she said. 'It was a non-starter. What time do you want me?'

8.45 a.m.

Tansy was waiting for Holly at the school gates.

'Just wait till you see Jade!' she began the moment her friend drew within earshot. 'You won't believe it!'

Holly frowned.

'What do you mean? Is she in a miff because she couldn't get tickets?'

Tansy grinned.

64

'Oh, she got them all right!' she laughed. 'And how!'

Oh, thought Holly. Now what do I do?

'Come on – she's over there by the cycle park.' She set off across the playground. 'Hey, Jade!'

A girl with short hair the colour of rusty nails turned round.

Holly stopped dead in her tracks.

'Jade? Jade!' she gasped. 'Your hair – it's gone.'

'Very observant,' said Jade. 'Do you like it?'

Holly swallowed.

'It's . . . well, it's . . . very striking,' she said, not wanting to be unkind. 'But why? I'd die to have hair like yours . . . like yours was.'

Now you tell me, thought Jade.

'I was fed up with looking like a nerdy kid,' said Jade abruptly, wishing that Holly had sounded more enthusiastic. 'By the way, here's your ticket.'

Holly looked at it with some reluctance. She couldn't give up a night with Paul, and yet it was only because of her that the others were going to the gig.

'Oh, thanks,' she said.

'Is that it?' muttered Jade. 'Aren't you impressed?'

Holly nodded.

'Yes, well done,' she said.

'I think', said Jade, 'it was the hair that clinched it.'

'I don't doubt it,' said Holly. 'Not for a moment.'

10.30 a.m. Looking for a way out

I could always say I got a migraine at the last

65

moment, thought Holly during Chemistry. They'd never know. And it wouldn't be like letting anyone down.

They'd have each other. I'll just ring Tansy at the last moment and sound ill. It won't matter.

11.15 a.m. Should I, shouldn't I?
Grounded or not, I have to get out tonight, thought Jade. There's no way I can miss Shiny Vinyl. Not that I'm that desperate, especially as Scott's not going. But the others will think I'm chicken. Besides, they won't get in without me.

I wish I'd never opened my mouth in the first place.

12.45 p.m. Forward planning over a pizza
'Right,' announced Tansy, as she tucked into a rapidly cooling slice of what the school called pizza. 'We need to get organized for tonight. I've told my mum we're going to the cinema and she said she'd drop me and Holly off. All we have to do is wait till she's gone and then zoom upstairs to The Danger Zone. Do you want a lift, Jade?'

Jade sighed.

'Right now, Paula is saying I can't go,' she said.

'Oh no!' gasped Tansy. 'You have to go – you're the one who's going to help bluff us all in.'

Jade fiddled with a piece of five-centimetre-long hair and thought yet again how bare she felt.

'Oh, don't worry,' she said, a lot more confidently

than she felt, 'I'll sort Paula. I'll meet you all there. What about you, Cleo?'

I really don't want to do this, thought Cleo, scoffing a Danish pastry. She always ate when under stress.

'I'm not sure,' she began. 'It's not really my sort of thing.'

'Oh, don't be a weed!' said Tansy airily. 'Chill out, Cleo. It'll be a laugh.'

2 p.m. Looking for guidance

Paula stood beside the telephone and lifted the receiver.

Had she been too hard? She so wanted Jade to love her, but she couldn't let her get away with ruining her looks like that. David had said she had been too hard on her niece but surely the other mothers would have put their foot down too? Quite apart from the hair business, it was a school night.

'Oh, get on with it,' she told herself irritably. 'Just do it.'

She dialled the number and waited. Eventually a somewhat weary voice at the other end announced that this was Dunchester 864535.

'Oh, Mrs Vine,' said Paula politely, 'this is Paula Webb, Jade's aunt . . . Yes, that's right.'

She took a deep breath.

'Look, Jade tells me that the girls want to go to the cinema tonight and well, I just wondered whether you really were going to let Holly go . . . You are?

But I thought with homework and everything . . .'

She listened as Angela Vine held forth at some length about letting children take responsibility for their lives and the benefits of social intercourse before saying a polite goodbye and hanging up.

She tried Clarity Meadows, who said of course Tansy was going, which didn't surprise Paula because she had always had her doubts about Clarity's suitability as a parent. When Clarity suggested giving Jade a lift, Paula refused at once. No way was she letting her niece go anywhere in anyone else's car. You couldn't be too careful.

'No thanks, I can arrange something,' Paula said hastily. No way was she letting Jade go anywhere in Clarity Meadow's disreputable van.

I'll have to let her go tonight, she thought, walking to the sink and filling the kettle. I just hope she'll be all right. She's so vulnerable. Not that I'm handling any of it properly. I just look at her and I think of her mum and I want so much to say the right things and I can't. The words don't come.

I love Jade so much and sometimes I think she hates me. Oh, Lizzie, why did you have to die?

4.30 p.m. Reprieved!
'Jade? Is that you?'

Paula came out of the sitting room into the hallway as Jade opened the front door.

'Look, about tonight . . .'

Here we go, thought Jade. Another battle royal.

68

'. . . maybe I was a bit over the top,' continued Paula hurriedly. 'I'm disgusted abut your hair – I think you were very foolish – but it's done now. You can go.'

Jade's face broke into a huge grin.

'Thanks, Paula. Thanks a lot.'

'But I'm taking you and fetching you,' she insisted firmly.

'Yes, Paula,' said Jade meekly.

She was going to Shiny Vinyl. Against all the odds, her street cred was intact for another day.

5.45 p.m. Sick note

'Dunchester five-double-seven-zero-seven-eight, Tansy here!'

'Tansy, it's me – Holly.'

'Oh, hiya,' said Tansy. 'I'm just deciding what to wear. Do you think the purple satin skirt or those red –'

'I'm ill. I can't come,' moaned Holly, crossing her fingers firmly behind her back and hoping she sounded at the point of expiry. 'I've got a migraine.'

Tansy gasped.

'Bad luck!' she said. 'And you were so looking forward to it.'

'I know,' sighed Holly. 'Must go. I'll be thinking of you.'

Not, thought Holly.

Wednesday

7.05 p.m. En route for disaster

'This is luxury!' said Tansy as she climbed into the Greenways' car. 'Thank goodness we didn't have to go in Mum's old van.'

'Sorry we're a bit late, Tansy!' said Cleo's mum as they drove away from her house. 'My agent phoned about the filming just as we were about to leave.'

Tansy looked impressed.

'Are you going to be in a film, Mrs Greenway?' she asked.

Diana laughed.

'I wish,' she said. 'No, I'm having a screen test to appear in a series of adverts for those nice knickers.'

Cleo cringed.

'Knickers?' queried Tansy.

'Yes, dear, I'm going . . .'

She frowned and pumped her foot up and down on the accelerator. 'What is wrong with this car? It's stopping.'

She steered the car on to the hard shoulder. It stopped.

'Mum!' exclaimed Cleo in exasperation. 'You've run out of petrol.'

Diana gazed at the petrol gauge as if it had personally insulted her.

'Well, how did that happen?' she asked.

'Probably by not filling the tank before you left,' said Cleo.

'Oh, this is too irritating for words!' exclaimed Diana, opening the car door and clambering out.

70

'And I've left my mobile phone at home.'

She stood at the edge of the roadside and began waving her arms in the air.

'Mum . . .' began Cleo.

'Don't worry, you won't miss the main film,' her mother replied. 'They always have adverts on for ages.'

Tansy and Cleo looked at one another. Never mind films. Shiny Vinyl were on in half an hour.

7.15 p.m. Be sure your sins
will find you out

'I'll meet you by the fountain at ten o'clock sharp,' said Paula. 'Be there.'

Jade ran into the cinema foyer and looked round for the others. She spotted Holly at the far side of the foyer talking to a guy Jade didn't recognize. Trust Holly to try chat-up lines at every opportunity.

'Hi, Holly! Come on, if we dash we'll just make it.'

Holly spun round and stared at Jade openmouthed.

'What are you doing here?' she said. 'You're supposed to be at the gig.'

'I thought you said it was a non-starter,' interrupted the guy. 'Hi, I'm Paul Bennett.'

Light began to dawn. Paul. The guy Holly fancied.

'Oh, great,' said Jade. 'So you're coming along too?' That would be good. He looked at least sixteen.

Paul looked bewildered.

'We're here to see *Spinnaker*.'

71

Holly was turning an interesting shade of puce and chewing her lip.

'Paul, can you just get me some popcorn? I'll be with you in a second.'

She lowered her voice as Paul moved away.

'Holly, what's going on?' demanded Jade.

'I had to come,' Holly said with a pleading note in her voice. 'I mean, he's to die for, and if I'd said no –'

'He'd have asked you another time!' snapped Jade. 'Just let down all your friends, why don't you?'

She needed Holly there. Jade might have the new hairdo but Holly had enough attitude for all of them.

'Jade, don't be like that. This is love. I mean, the Real Thing. Like you and Scott.'

Huh! thought Jade. Scott isn't exactly pining to be with me every hour of the day.

'Look,' said Holly, as Paul reappeared with the popcorn, 'you'd better go and find the others. See you!'

And she dragged Paul off towards the entrance to Screen Two.

Jade was furious. How could Holly do this? And where were the others? She scanned the foyer but there was no sign of Cleo or Tansy.

Maybe they thought they were meeting upstairs at The Danger Zone. She'd just have to go there and hope they were waiting.

7.29 p.m. Going it alone

'Are you coming in or not?' The bouncer on the door

was getting impatient. 'Once the band are on, we're closing the doors.'

Jade bit her lip. Maybe Cleo and Tansy were already inside. She'd murder Holly for this.

She waved her ticket in the man's face and was smugly satisfied to see that he didn't even blink an eye. She pushed through the doors and into the club. The lights were dim and the floor was a heaving mass of bodies. The warm-up band were thundering out a rock number as Jade tried desperately to spot her friends.

'Hi, sweetheart!' A tall guy with long hair and three nose studs laid a hand on her shoulder. Jade jumped, glared at him and pushed her way further through the throng. Everyone seemed much older than her, and several of them were smoking and swigging beer from cans. Jade felt very self-conscious.

Everyone was pressing closer and closer to the stage. Maybe Tansy and Cleo had grabbed some good places. She edged her way nearer.

As she did so she brushed against a girl in a short black skirt and lime-green halter neck, gyrating in the arms of a broad-shouldered guy with floppy ginger hair.

It couldn't be.

It was.

Oh no!

She turned round to escape but someone bumped into her and she lost her footing, falling against the brown-haired girl as she did so.

'Hey, look where you're . . . Jade!'

It was too late. She'd seen her. Now she'd be for it. Most of her mates would keep their mouths shut.

But not her cousin Allegra.

7.30 p.m. Havoc on the hard shoulder

Cleo thought she would die of embarrassment. Her mother was not fit to be allowed out on her own. She had actually stood at the side of the road, and started jumping up and down, waving her arms in the air at every passing motorist. After a few moments, a blue Granada had pulled up and Mrs Greenway had run up to the driver's door, wiggling her bottom in her white Levis and beaming.

'I've been such a silly!' she shrilled in the sort of voice she had used when playing in Jeeves and Wooster. 'Could you possibly sort me out?'

'I'll sort her out if she carries on like that,' muttered Cleo to Tansy, as the driver wound down his window.

'Cleo! Look who it is!' Tansy burst into a fit of giggles.

Cleo peered through the windscreen. Heaving himself out of the driving seat and eyeing Diana Greenway with unnecessary interest was Mr Grubb.

'Beetle!' gasped Cleo. 'I can't bear it!'

'I think I'm out of petrol,' Diana was saying. 'Oh, Mr Grubb, dear, it's you!'

Cleo closed her eyes. What was she thinking of?

'Mrs Greenway!' beamed Mr Grubb. 'Girls!'

Tansy and Cleo gave him a sick sort of grin.

'Well now,' he said briskly. 'Not to worry. We'll siphon off a bit of petrol from my car.'

'You are a positive angel!' simpered Diana, flicking her hand through her hair in an actressy sort of way and smiling coyly.

'Only too pleased to help a star of stage and screen!' rejoined Mr Grubb, turning an interesting shade of ripe tomato. 'And what theatrical gem are you working on now?'

'I think', Cleo muttered to Tansy, 'I am about to throw up.'

Diana cocked her head to one side.

'Well,' she said, 'I hope to be doing a series of TV adverts, actually.'

'Indeed?' said Beetle, feeding the hose into the petrol inlet. 'And what delight will you be selling us?'

'Knickers,' giggled Diana.

Cleo cringed. Had her mother no shame at all? It was bad enough to contemplate such behaviour, without telling the entire world about it.

'They say I have the right bottom for it,' Diana added.

'Tansy,' said Cleo.

'Yes?'

'Tell me I'm dreaming. Tell me she didn't say that.'

Tansy grinned.

'I think it's wonderful,' she said.

Cleo gazed at her.

'Wonderful? You're mad.'

Tansy shook her head.

'It's a total relief to know that it isn't just my mum who is certifiable.'

7.35 p.m. Double take

Allegra stared at Jade.

Jade stared at Allegra.

'What are you doing here?' demanded Allegra. 'I thought you were supposed to be at the cinema.'

'And I thought you were supposed to be on a theatre trip,' rejoined Jade.

They stared at one another again.

'If you tell, I'll never ever speak to you again,' snapped Allegra.

'Tempting as that offer is,' said Jade, 'I am hardly likely to, am I?'

'You're not?'

Jade shook her head.

'Because if I did, she'd know I was here too, wouldn't she?'

They both began to smile.

'Mum would kill me if she found out,' said Allegra. 'She used to be quite laid-back but lately she's got really uptight.'

Jade nodded.

'Tell me about it,' she said. 'She almost hyperventilated at the thought of me going to the cinema.'

Hugo shuffled at the side of her.

'Are we dancing or what?' he said.

'In a minute. Oh, this is Jade – you know, the cousin I was telling you about?'

Hugo eyed her with interest.

'Oh, hi! She doesn't look like a dweeb to me,' he added, turning to Allegra.

Allegra had the good grace to blush.

'She's not really,' she said hastily. 'She's improving.'

'Oh, thanks,' said Jade sarcastically.

The warm-up band were leaving the stage and everyone began pushing towards the front to get the best positions to hear Shiny Vinyl.

'Who are you with?' asked Allegra. 'Scott?'

Jade shook her head and told Allegra the whole story.

'So ... you mean Mum is picking you up? Downstairs? But the gig ends at ten o'clock as well.'

'So?'

'What if she sees me? Hannah's mum is meeting us at the fountain too. Everyone meets there.'

Allegra nibbled a fingernail and looked anxious.

At that moment, Shiny Vinyl came on stage. Everyone surged forward as they struck up the first number. Jade was squashed against Allegra and a huge girl with dangly earrings and BO.

For the next twenty minutes, Jade couldn't make herself heard above the noise. It wasn't her sort of music and she was beginning to feel a bit panicky as people kept shoving and pushing against her. She turned to speak to Allegra and found that she had been pushed several metres away.

She was beginning to wish she hadn't come when a tall guy shot out his arm in time to the music and spilt beer all down her skirt.

'Oh no!' she gasped involuntarily. Now what? Paula would smell it a mile off. She just wanted to get out of there. It was smelly and hot, and she was getting a cracking headache and feeling queasy.

She glanced across to where Allegra was swaying to the beat, waving her arms in the air and clearly having a great time. If I tell her I'm going home, she'll think I'm a no-hoper, she thought. Mind you, if she starts picking on me I can always threaten to drop her in it.

That gave Jade an idea.

The band was coming to the end of the second number, and Jade took the chance to shove her way through to reach her cousin.

'Yuk!' said Allegra. 'You stink!'

'Precisely,' moaned Jade. 'Paula will suss immediately that I didn't get like this watching a film. And of course, if she does see you . . .'

Allegra pulled a face.

'Don't even talk about it,' she said.

'So', said Jade, trying to sound as if she was doing Allegra a huge favour, 'I'm going home. I'll sponge my skirt down in the loo and then tell Paula I was sick or something. That way, I'm in the clear, she won't turn out to pick me up and you'll be off the hook as well.'

Allegra had watched her with ever-widening eyes as she spoke.

'That's a cool idea,' she said admiringly. 'But what about the gig? They're playing their number-one hit later on.'

Jade shrugged.

'I'm not that bothered about Shiny Vinyl,' she said. 'I only did it to prove that I'm my own person and not some nerdy kid to be bossed about. Just remember that, right?'

Allegra grinned and nodded.

'I don't reckon', she said, 'that I'm likely to forget that in a hurry. I'll see you later. And Jade . . .'

'Yes.'

'I owe you one.'

9 p.m. The best-laid plans . . .

'Paula,' she called, 'it's me – Jade.'

Paula emerged from the sitting room looking rather red-eyed and clutching a scrunched-up tissue.

'Jade?' she said, with a watery smile. 'What are you doing back so soon? And your skirt . . .'

'I was sick,' said Jade.

'Oh dear . . .' began Paula, looking anxious.

'Could you pay the taxi? I didn't have enough.'

Paula opened the front door.

'How much?' she called to the driver.

'Four pounds fifty,' he shouted back.

'That seems an awful lot,' said Paula.

'Well, you see, luv, it's that new one-way system. From The Danger Zone you have to go all round the houses to get out of the town centre.'

Please don't let her have heard that, God. Please.

It seemed God was not listening. Paula virtually threw the money at the taxi driver and rounded on Jade.

'The Danger Zone!' she exploded, grabbing her elbow and propelling her back into the house. 'That sleazy down-at-heel dump in the Rainbow Centre? You went *there*?'

Jade decided to brazen it out.

'So what if I did?' she retorted. 'I'm home, aren't I? You want me to grow up. That's what I'm doing.'

Paula narrowed her eyes.

'You can grow up without going to places like that!' she stormed. 'Anything could have happened.'

'But it didn't,' said Jade.

'Well, something must have done for you to have got a cab home,' replied Paula. 'Have you been drinking? Is that it?'

'No it is not!' shouted Jade. 'Why do you always think badly of me?'

Paula put her hands to her head.

'I don't ... it's just ... you've changed, Jade. First this awful hair business and now going to the sort of place none of my kids would even think of frequenting ...'

Jade wanted to tell her. To prove that she wasn't

the only one fed up with being told what to do. Why should she take all the blame? But then, dropping Allegra in it wouldn't be fair and besides, there was nothing Paula could do to her now.

'Well, you obviously need to be taught a lesson,' announced Paula. 'You are not going on this activity weekend and that is final.'

Jade stared at her. She couldn't mean it. She had to go.

'That's not fair!' she began. 'Everyone's going.'

'Everyone', said Paula, 'except you. You have only yourself to blame. What's more, I shall go and see the head first thing tomorrow. Now go to bed.'

She marched back into the sitting room and slammed the door.

'I hate you!' shouted Jade. 'I really, really hate you!'

She turned and ran up the stairs, tears welling up in her eyes, and flung open her bedroom door.

And stopped dead.

Standing by her bed, in a pink Winnie the Pooh dressing gown, was Nell. And in her hands was Jade's silver money box. And it was open.

'Don't tell, please don't tell!' the little girl whispered after Jade had removed the box and found three one-pound coins in Nell's dressing-gown pocket. 'I only borrowed it.'

Jade sat down beside her and put an arm round her shoulders.

81

'But why?' she asked. 'You have your own money – remember all that money you got from the grannies for your birthday?'

Nell sniffed.

'It's all gone,' she said.

Jade frowned.

'It can't have,' she protested. 'What did you buy?'

'Nuffin,' said Nell.

Jade was tired, fed up and furious with Paula for being so mean. She didn't mean to snap but she couldn't help it.

'Oh, for heaven's sake, Nell,' she said. 'You've either spent it or you've got it. And either way you don't go round taking what doesn't belong to you. Now give it back and go to bed!'

Nell rammed her thumb into her mouth and shuffled off the bed.

'And don't you ever do that again!' Jade said. 'Because next time I will tell!'

'That was pretty nice of you,' said Allegra an hour later, after she had woken Jade up by crashing into the bedroom and switching on all the lights. 'Thanks.'

Jade yawned.

'I hope it was worth it,' she said.

'Course it was – the band was mega brilliant and Hugo kissed me. Twice. Life can't get any better than this.'

Jade sighed.

'Mine can't get any worse,' she said.

'Oh, Jade, don't start on about death again. Please.'

Jade shook her head.

'I'm not,' she said. 'It's Paula. She's grounded me for going to The Danger Zone. The taxi driver let it slip. She's even stopping me from going to Sussex.'

'Oh no!' exclaimed Allegra. 'She can't do that! It's not fair.'

Allegra cares about *me*? thought Jade in surprise.

'You *have* to go away this weekend. I've asked Hannah to sleep over. We need your bed.'

'Oh, great,' said Jade, coming back to reality. 'Thanks a million.'

THURSDAY

'So what happened to you last night?' Jade accosted Tansy and Cleo as soon as they walked into the classroom.

Cleo looked apologetic.

'My mum's car ran out of petrol,' she said.

'Oh yes?' retorted Jade, who could only stop herself from crying by being snappy. 'That's about as feeble an excuse as Holly's migraine.'

'What do you mean?' asked Tansy, frowning.

'Holly was at the Multiscreen last night. With Paul.'

'She wasn't? Really? So you were at The Danger Zone on your own?'

Jade nodded.

'Thanks to you,' she said.

'Honestly, Jade, the car did run out of petrol,'

84

Tansy said. 'Ask Beetle. He came to Mrs Greenway's rescue. I think he fancies her.'

'Who fancies who?' Holly appeared at Tansy's elbow.

Jade turned to face her.

'How's the migraine, Holly?' she asked.

Holly blushed.

'OK, OK, so I lied,' she said. 'But it was worth it. Paul's so gorgeous. And I shall have him for three whole days at the centre. I can't wait to get there, can you?'

'I'm not going,' said Jade, with a catch in her voice.

The three stared at her.

'What do you mean?' gasped Cleo.

'I'm grounded. And it's all your fault. I hope you're all satisfied.'

10.45 a.m. Feelings of guilt

'Well, it's not our fault Cleo's mum ran out of petrol,' Tansy insisted. 'But you shouldn't have ditched Jade just because you had a better offer. If you'd been there, she wouldn't have gone home early and she wouldn't be grounded now.'

Holly looked abject.

'I know, I'm sorry,' she said. 'Do you really think Mrs Webb will stop Jade going to Sussex?'

Tansy shrugged.

'Sounds like it,' she said. 'Cleo saw her going into Plank's study when she was fetching some graph paper.'

Holly took a deep breath.

'Maybe we should do something.'

'WE?' chorused Tansy and Cleo in unison.

'OK then, me,' said Holly.

10.50 a.m. Head to head

'Mrs Webb, how nice to see you. Do please sit down.'

Mr Boardman gestured to an ancient leather arm-chair.

'Now what can I do for you?'

Paula took a deep breath.

'It's Jade,' she said. 'I'm afraid I've said she can no longer go on the school trip.'

The headmaster clasped his hands together, inclined his head enquiringly to one side and said nothing.

'She's been very defiant lately,' Paula continued, fiddling self-consciously with an earring. 'She went against my instructions and had this terrible hair-cut . . .'

'Ah yes, the hair,' murmured Mr Boardman. 'I had spotted that. A little alarming, isn't it?'

Paula nodded.

'Frightful,' she said. 'And then last night she told me she was going to the cinema and ended up at The Danger Zone, which she knew I wouldn't approve of.'

'Dear me,' said Mr Boardman, as mildly as if Paula had announced that Jade had nipped into Safeways for a can of lemonade.

'So I told her straight that it wasn't good enough

and the weekend trip was off,' concluded Paula.

'I see,' murmured Mr Boardman.

'I'm glad you agree,' said Paula, picking up her bag.

'Oh, but I don't,' said the headmaster.

Paula looked at him in amazement.

'You don't?'

'Oh no,' he said. 'Everything you have told me points to just one thing.'

'What?' demanded Paula.

'That Jade must most definitely come on the school trip.'

10.55 a.m. Perfect prose

'Will this do?' Holly shoved a piece of paper under Tansy's nose.

Dear Mrs Webb,

I know that Jade is in trouble for going to The Danger Zone but the only reason you found out was because I let her down, and she was fed up and decided to go home early. Please let her come on the activity weekend – she's one of my best friends and, besides, she's had a rough time lately and it will cheer her up. By the way, she doesn't know I am writing this so please don't think she set me up.

Yours very sincerely and in hopeful anticipation,
Holly Vine

'I thought the hopeful anticipation bit had rather a nice ring to it,' she observed.

'It's good,' conceded Tansy. 'How will you get it to her?'

'She must still be with Mr Boardman,' said Holly. 'I'll hand it to Reception and they can give it to her when she hands back her security pass.'

'That's brilliant!' said Tansy.

'I know,' said Holly.

10.57 a.m. Head lines

'So you see, Mrs Webb, this sort of weekend is just what Jade needs. She has to express her grief and her frustrations and obviously she is finding that hard to do at home.'

Paula flung him an angry stare.

'So you're saying I'm not providing her with the right environment, not being loving enough, not –'

Mr Boardman held up his hand.

'Mrs Webb, I'm saying nothing of the sort. But you must be suffering too. The loss of a sister is a terrible thing.'

To Paula's horror, she felt her eyes filling with tears. She grabbed a tissue from her handbag.

'Death affects people in so many different ways,' said Mr Boardman calmly, pretending not to notice Paula's distress. 'Some of us get angry, others try to pretend it never happened and bury it deep inside. But for everyone, it must come out some time, some way.'

He paused.

'Can I get you a glass of water?'

'I'm fine,' Paula said hurriedly. 'It's not easy taking another child into the family, but I love her, and I do want the best for her.'

Mr Boardman smiled.

'Then trust me. Send her to Downsview with us. You'll be surprised at what it does for her.'

11.05 a.m. Touch lines

Paula strode across the car park and opened the door of her Metro. Slumping down in the driver's seat, she leaned back, closed her eyes and took a deep breath.

Fancy almost making a fool of herself like that. She was over all the weeping bit.

She'd put it all behind her. Hadn't she?

She tore open the letter that the receptionist had handed to her. As she scanned the contents, her eyes filled with tears again.

Jade had a friend rooting for her. A friend who was prepared to own up for her sake. Even if the head-master hadn't persuaded her to change her mind, that letter would have done.

Turning the key in the ignition, she reversed the car out of the car park.

'Oh, Lizzie,' she said, biting her lip. 'I miss you so much.'

And this time, the tears did fall.

4.00 p.m. The bottom line

'Do you think you have to do *every* activity?' Cleo asked Trig anxiously as they walked home together.

'I doubt it,' said Trig. 'I reckon if you find one you're good at, they'd let you stick at that.'

'I won't be good at any of it,' moaned Cleo. 'I'll be totally useless and everyone will laugh.'

Trig turned to face her.

'I won't laugh,' he said. 'I'm dreading it too.'

Cleo wanted to hug him. Most guys would have pretended to be mega macho but Trig was so upfront.

'Do you want to come in for a bit?' suggested Cleo as they reached her house.

'OK,' said Trig. 'But not for long. I have to pack.'

Cleo unlocked the front door.

'Come through and get a drink,' she said. 'Then we could –'

'TA-RAR!' The lounge door flew open and Diana Greenway leapt out, arms outstretched in dancer mode. 'What do you think, darling?'

She wriggled her bottom.

'How could they choose anyone else? I reckon it's a – oh. Ah. Hello, Trig.'

Cleo stood stock still. Behind her Trig swallowed and turned his eyes to examine the watercolour hanging on the wall.

Mrs Greenway was dressed in a pair of lilac knickers, adorned with small green frogs. She had on a matching bra. And nothing else.

Since she was an actress and, thought Cleo, a woman totally without shame, her mum recovered immediately.

'Fittinix – Your Firmup Friend,' she trilled, whipping a raincoat off the hall coat-stand and wrapping it over her shoulders. 'Such fun!'

And with that she ran upstairs, still giggling.

'You know,' said Cleo, 'I am looking forward to this weekend after all.'

'You are?' queried Trig in surprise.

'Yes,' said Cleo. 'Anything has to be an improvement on living with a manic mother.'

4.15 p.m. 53 Lime Avenue. Saying nothing
There's Jade now, thought Paula as the front door slammed. I've got to get this right. Please let me say it right.

'Hello, darling,' she said brightly. 'Look, I went to see Mr Boardman,' she began.

'Oh, terrific,' muttered Jade. 'I suppose you sat there and told each other what was wrong with me.'

'No, darling, actually he . . . I . . . we decided you should go on this weekend trip,' she said.

Jade's face lit up.

'Really? Oh, thanks, Paula!'

'Wait – I haven't finished.'

I have to talk about Lizzie. I have to tell her that I'm hurting too. I can't. I'll cry. And that wouldn't help her at all, would it?

'Yes?' urged Jade.

'Nothing.'

5.00 p.m. Saying even less

Jade was finishing her packing and wondering whether her lilac strappy slip dress would be too over the top for the disco, when she heard Nell talking to herself in the next room.

She frowned, crept on to the landing and peeped round Nell's door.

Nell was sitting on her bed, with a doll in her lap. And she was shaking it furiously.

'You stupid little kid! Baby! Little wimp!'

'Nell!' Jade exclaimed. 'What *are* you doing?'

Nell looked up, pressed her lips together and said nothing.

And suddenly Jade knew. She was absolutely certain. She looked at the little girl's face and saw the fear in her eyes.

'Nell, someone is being horrible to you, aren't they?' she said. 'And they've told you not to tell.'

Nell's eyes widened and Jade could see the battle going on inside her head.

'Well, that's OK,' she said, 'because you haven't told me, have you? I've guessed. So when you're ready to give me some more clues, you do that.'

Nell's eyes filled with tears. She took a deep breath.

Now she'll tell me, thought Jade.

'Yes,' she urged. 'Who is it? Who's being horrid?'

'No one,' said Nell.

FRIDAY

11 a.m. Here we go, here we go, here we go

'Why are we waiting? Why-I are we waiting?'

The coach was stuck in a queue of traffic in Brighton and several of the boys had started chanting in impatience.

Jade had her nose glued to the window. The nearer they had got to Brighton, the more memories had come flooding back. Jack and Jill windmills where they used to go for picnics when she was small; the Brendon riding stables where she had fallen off Toffee the Shetland pony and knocked out her front tooth.

'That's where I used to live! Look, up there!'

The coach was gathering speed as they passed the bottom of Kemp Hill. Jade craned her neck to catch sight of her old house but a lorry overtaking them got in the way.

'And my gran lives round that corner!' she said, although no one was taking much notice.

The only other person who was taking any interest in what was going on out of the coach window was Andy. He didn't say a word, but Tansy, who was observing him closely, had a pretty good idea what he was thinking.

She wished she could conjure his mother up out of thin air, if only to take the sadness out of his eyes.

11.30 a.m. Arrival at Downsview

'It's massive!' Holly breathed as the coach turned through wrought-iron gates and up the gravelled driveway of the Downsview Centre.

Ahead of them stood a rambling grey stone house with turrets at either end and dozens of mullioned windows glinting in the sun. In front of the house was a wide expanse of lawn dotted with croquet hoops, and to the side lay tennis courts and another lawn with archery targets at the far end.

'Look at that lake!' said Scott. 'It's huge!'

'That's Pitsley Reservoir', said Miss Partridge, 'where some of you will have the chance to try canoeing and dinghy sailing.'

A number of butterflies gathered in the pit of Cleo's stomach.

'And just beyond are Weir Rocks,' interjected Mr Grubb enthusiastically. 'That's where you shall be going for climbing and abseiling.'

The butterflies took on new recruits and assembled for action.

'Right, everyone,' said Miss Partridge, clapping her

94

hands, 'here we are at Downsview. Bishop Agnew College have rooms in the main building and we are in the Stable Block. A quick lunch and then off to your first challenge. Dinghy sailing for Group A . . .'

Cleo's butterflies took off and flew in formation. She wished she had never come.

2.00 p.m. I am sailing, I am . . .

'It's awfully windy, isn't it?' said Cleo nervously as they stood at the edge of the reservoir after the first hour of their basic on-shore training.

'It has to be for sailing,' said Holly, scanning the group of Bishop Agnew kids who were already on the water in dinghies. 'There's Paul – look!'

'Right,' said Graham, the senior instructor. 'These little Toppers are what everyone learns to sail in.'

He gestured to what appeared to be a floating soap dish.

'What – on our own?' gasped Cleo.

Graham grinned.

'John and Tim here will be in rescue boats at your side – no harm can come to you. Now, who's going first?'

'Me!' cried Holly. She could just imagine herself whipping over the waves and coming alongside Paul, whose eyes would light up with love and passion.

She stepped into the tiny little dinghy and one of the instructors climbed into the motorized rescue boat.

'Right, three more volunteers, please – Cleo, Trig and Ursula!'

Cleo felt sick.

'I'm scared,' she said to Holly as she clambered clumsily into the boat.

'Don't be,' said Holly. 'I'll be nearby.'

This is meant to make me feel better? wondered Cleo.

One of the junior instructors pushed her off from the shingle shoreline. The wind caught the small sail and the little boat gathered speed.

Holly was trying to keep an eye on Paul's boat but the sun was in her eyes and she couldn't really see where she was going. It did feel very unstable. She tried to remember what the instructor had told her. Maybe she should lean the other way.

There again . . . perhaps not.

She looked wildly round to see where the others were. Not that she was scared or anything – just to reassure Cleo that everything was OK. Cleo was bowling along in a straight line, her face screwed up in concentration, and there was another, larger dinghy, coming towards her. Very fast. How did you move these things out of the way?

Which rope was she meant to pull? This one?

She tugged on the mainsheet and the little boat leaned.

The other boat got nearer. It was Paul. He'd obviously seen her. Her heart pounded.

He was leaning back off the side of the boat, like

the pictures she had seen in magazines, looking lean and athletic.

She adopted the same pose, hoping she looked sporty and rather sultry.

Out of the corner of her eye she could see the instructor waving at her from the rescue boat.

She waved back.

The boat leaned. Holly tried to sit up. And slipped.

The water was very cold. As she struggled to the surface, spitting a strand of green weed from her mouth, she saw two faces peering down at her.

One was the instructor, looking a little anxious. The other was Paul. And he was laughing hysterically.

3.00 p.m.

Jade and the pony eyed one another closely. It was difficult to tell who was the more suspicious.

Scott was already sitting casually on top of a chestnut pony with milky eyes and a bored expression, and several Bishop Agnew kids were filing off across the field. She couldn't put it off any longer.

The instructor gave her a leg-up and Jade clutched the reins. It seemed an awfully long way up.

'I'll take you on the lead rein for a bit,' said the instructor. 'Just till you get the hang of it.'

The countryside was beautiful. Gradually Jade began to relax and look at the scenery around her. In the distance the sea glimmered in the late afternoon sun and she could hear the faint cry of angry seagulls cresting the air currents.

It was as they crossed the country lane outside the Centre that Jade spotted the sign – Cycle track: Brighton four miles.

Four miles! That was hardly any distance. She wished she had her bike with her. She hadn't ridden it much since moving to Dunchester because Paula worried about traffic and accidents, but she was pretty fit and it wouldn't have taken her any time at all to get into the town. Not that she would have been allowed out.

She sighed. She did want to see her old house. If she closed her eyes she could picture her mother standing in the tiny front garden, fussing over her hollyhocks and delphiniums, and hear her dad teasing and saying that anyone would think it was Kew Gardens, the time she spent in it. Jade's mum always said that if she couldn't have a country cottage, at least she could have a cottage garden. The very day she was killed, she had planted a new rose bush that Dad had given her for an anniversary present. Elizabeth of Glamis, it was called, but Dad had changed the label and written 'Lizzie of My Heart', which Jade thought was so romantic for an old person.

'Right,' said the instructor, breaking into her thoughts, 'we'll try a trot.'

After that there was no time for thinking about roses or anything else.

3.30 p.m. *Mission accomplished*

'I can't believe I survived that,' said Cleo to Trig as they hauled the boats ashore.

'It was cool,' agreed Trig.

'It was terrifying,' protested Cleo. 'But at least I'm in one piece, unlike poor Holly. She does look a bit bedraggled.'

'Who's the guy with her?' asked Trig.

'I think it must be Paul,' said Cleo. 'She really fancies him. I bet she's dying of shame.'

3.32 p.m. *Truth time*

'I thought', Paul was saying to Holly, 'that you could sail?'

'So I lied,' muttered Holly, mortified at having made a fool of herself in front of the one guy she needed to impress.

'You do a lot of that, don't you?' said Paul.

Holly looked abject.

'Only teasing,' he said. 'Are you OK?'

Holly nodded.

'I can't see what went wrong,' she said. 'You leaned back out of your boat and nothing happened.'

Paul burst out laughing.

'You really don't know a thing about sailing, do you?' he said. 'Mine was a Laser and I had a harness on. You don't do that sort of thing in a Topper.'

'I don't think', said Holly ruefully, 'that I shall do anything in any sort of boat ever again.'

Friday

6.00 p.m. Evening agony

'I don't think', said Jade to Tansy as they filed into supper, 'that I shall ever sit down in comfort again.'

'Tell me about it,' grinned Tansy. 'I did rock climbing with Andy and my neck is killing me.'

'Your neck?' interjected Cleo, who was wondering whether there were any totally safe activities left to try the next day. 'You don't use your neck to hold a rope.'

Tansy grinned.

'I kept looking up at Andy's legs,' she said. 'He does have lovely thighs, you know.'

Holly sighed.

'Paul has lovely everything,' she said, 'but he will probably never speak to me again. Fate is very cruel.'

Jade and Cleo exchanged a wry smile. Holly's immersion in Pitsley Reservoir had done nothing to dampen down her sense of the dramatic.

6.05 p.m. Failed connections

Jade fed her money into the payphone and dialled her grandmother's number.

The phone rang and rang. No reply. Maybe Gran's flight had been delayed. Or maybe the plane had crashed and Gran was . . . No, that was silly. Gran would be fine. Jade just hoped she would get the chance to try calling her again.

11.00 p.m. Creepy conversation

The four girls lay in their sleeping bags in the darkened room.

'Do you think', asked Holly sleepily, 'that this place is haunted?'

'Could be,' agreed Tansy. 'The house is very old.'

'But this is the stable block,' said Cleo, who didn't enjoy talk of ghosts. 'So it won't be.'

'It might,' persisted Holly. 'Maybe one of the grooms had a secret love affair with the mistress of the house and was banished for ever and now he roams what used to be the tack room in search of his forbidden love.'

'Or', continued Tansy, taking up the theme, 'the lord of the manor is so furious that his house has been turned into an activity centre for modern kids that he paces the place every night intent on wreaking havoc.'

Cleo wriggled further down into her sleeping bag.

'Do you think dead people really do come back?' she whispered in a rather small voice.

'I wish they did,' said Jade.

After that no one said any more about ghosts.

1.30 a.m. Bad dreams

A loud scream woke Tansy and Jade with a start. It was Cleo.

'Cleo, Cleo, wake up, you're dreaming!' Tansy shook her arm.

Cleo opened her eyes.

'Oh sorry, sorry, I . . .' Tears were pouring down her face.

'Did you have a nightmare?' asked Tansy anxiously.

'I'll put the light on,' said Jade, wriggling out of her sleeping bag.

Holly snored on oblivious.

Cleo shook her head and wiped her eyes on the corner of her pyjama jacket.

'No, don't, I'm fine,' she assured her. 'Silly of me. Sorry.'

'There's nothing silly about dreams,' said Jade. 'I have them all the time.'

Tansy nodded.

'They're supposed to be very good for you.'

This kind of good I can do without, thought Cleo, lying down and trying to blank out the terrifying images. It was as she was beginning to fall asleep that she realized that her worst fear had come true. She'd had a nightmare in front of her friends. And none of them seemed the slightest bit fazed.

SATURDAY

10.30 a.m. Feeling terrified

Cleo was halfway up a rock and didn't dare look down to see how far she had come, or up to see how far there was still to go. Her arms ached and her head was spinning. Above her Trig was laughing. Below her Tansy was telling everyone that this was mega. Why am I the only one who wishes she wasn't here? she thought, hanging on for dear life.

11.45 a.m. Feeling resigned

'Oh, very Maid Marion!' giggled Tansy as Cleo picked up an arrow and aimed it at the target.

I'll be useless at this too, thought Cleo.

'You go first,' she said to Tansy.

Tansy let fly an arrow. It veered off at an angle and disappeared behind a laurel bush.

Oh well, thought Cleo, it won't just be me that messes up this time. Here goes.

Saturday

1.00 p.m. Feeling smug

By lunchtime, Cleo was elated. She'd done it! She'd found something she was good at.

OK, so archery wasn't a daredevil sport and it probably wasn't very sexy. But she could do it! Miss Partridge had been very impressed when all Cleo's arrows hit the target. Tansy spent the whole hour in the bushes hunting for hers although the fact that Andy was doing the same thing probably had something to do with it. Cleo had done better than anyone. She felt she could take on the world.

1.25 p.m. Escape route

Halfway through lunch, Mr Grubb rapped on the table and asked for silence.

'This afternoon', he said, 'you have four hours of free time. Not for idling about, mind you. You can canoe, play croquet, take a mountain bike along the cycle tracks . . .'

Jade stopped, her forkful of apple crumble poised in mid-air.

Bikes. Four hours was quite a long time.

'No one is to leave the site and I want you all back here by six o'clock sharp.'

Yes, but he'd never know if she left the site, would he? Not if she was really careful. Could she do it? If she got found out, she'd be in big trouble. But by then, she would have been able to talk to her gran and persuaded her to let her come back and live with her. And all the trouble in the world was worth that.

She'd do it. She wouldn't tell anyone, not even Scott. This was something she had to do completely on her own.

2 p.m. Caught in the act

It had been surprisingly easy to slip out of the grounds. Jade had ridden a couple of times round the garden track and then dodged behind some big clumps of rhododendrons until the other bikers had headed off on one of the three tracks. Then she pushed the bike through a gap in the hedge and on to the road.

She rammed her denim jacket in the saddle bag and stopped to adjust the strap on her safety helmet.

'Where are you off to?'

The voice behind her caused her to jump out of her skin. She turned, her heart pounding. It was Andy.

'Oh, it's you!' she exclaimed in relief. 'I'm . . . er . . . I'm just looking for the cycle track.'

Andy grinned.

'And I'm looking for wild elephants,' he said. 'Where are you really going?'

Jade sighed.

'You won't let on? You have to promise.'

'On my mother's life,' said Andy.

'Don't ever, ever say that!' shouted Jade, and Andy stepped back in surprise. 'You don't know what you're saying.'

Andy's eyes dropped.

'Actually I do,' he said quietly. 'I'm sorry if I was tactless. I forgot about your parents. But my mum disappeared and I haven't seen her for a year.'

Jade gulped.

'I didn't know,' she said. 'I'm sorry.'

And she told him her plan.

'I was trying to find a bus stop,' said Andy, pulling the postcard from his jeans' pocket. 'Mum sent this – it's from Brighton – and then when we came here instead of Dorset it seemed like an omen and I just thought, maybe . . .'

His voice trailed off.

'Go on, tell me I'm stupid.'

Jade shook her head.

'You're not – but I guess there won't be many buses on a country lane like this.'

She made a quick decision.

'Get a bike and come with me. I'll wait for you round the corner.'

2.45 p.m.

The ride into Brighton had been easy. Most of it had been downhill or on the flat and once they hit the town centre, there were marked cycle paths which meant they didn't have to worry about the traffic.

'I'm going to walk along the seafront,' said Andy. 'Just in case.'

Jade nodded.

'Suppose we meet back here at half-past four. That should give us heaps of time to cycle back.'

106

Andy nodded and climbed back on his bike.

'I hope you find your mum,' she said.

'I don't expect I will, but I had to try,' said Andy. 'Do you know what I mean?'

Jade smiled.

'Yes,' she said, 'I know exactly what you mean.'

2.55 p.m. *Memories are made of this*

Jade turned the corner into Kemp Hill and jumped off her bike, looking expectantly up at number eight. And stopped stock still in the middle of the road.

'No!' she cried out loud. 'No!'

Gone was her mother's immaculate little garden. Gone was the white-painted gate and the chain-link fence. Instead of the crowded flower bed and a pocket-sized lawn, there was a stretch of cream paving slabs and one solitary tub of flowers. A rusting bicycle leaned against the wall and a child's doll with one arm missing lay abandoned by three empty milk bottles. All that was left was the rose bush Dad had given Mum, standing bedraggled by the front gate.

She went to take a closer look. And caught her breath. Hanging from the stem, faded and torn, was a label.

She fingered it.

'Lizzie of My Heart. All my love, darling, Robert.'

Jade's heart missed a beat. Her chest ached. She couldn't even cry.

'Oh, Dad,' she whispered. 'Oh, Mum.'

She crept up to the front window and peered in. The carpet and curtains were still the same. But now there was striped wallpaper and a posh border, and the wonky bookshelves which Dad had put up two Christmases ago had been taken down and a pine bookcase stood in their place.

She was just wondering whether she dared peep through the letter box when she heard voices behind her.

'Hey, Faith, who's that?'

'Excuse me, but what do you think you are doing?' A hand landed on Jade's shoulder and, with a jolt, she spun round.

A tall girl of about fifteen with auburn hair in a ponytail was regarding her severely.

'Sorry,' Jade muttered. 'I was . . . just looking.'

'Oh, and you make a habit of peering into other people's houses, do you?' retorted the girl with her.

Jade knew that voice. She turned.

'Tanya!'

The girl stared at her.

'Do I know . . . Jade! I didn't recognize you! Your hair!'

Jade shrugged.

'I know, I know, not my best decision,' she said. 'Oh, it's so good to see you! How are you?'

'Fine,' said Tanya. 'Faith, this is Jade. You know, I told you about her. She used to live in your house.'

Jade gasped.

'You live here?' she said. 'So it's your family that have absolutely ruined the garden.'

The girl nodded and gave a wry smile.

'I know, it is a shame, isn't it?' she said.

'A shame?' cried Jade. 'My mum worked flat out on that garden. She loved it. This concrete – it's horrid!'

Tanya laid a hand on her arm.

'OK, Jade, don't go on!' she said. 'It's not your house any more. They can do whatever they like with it. And they had a good reason.'

Jade glowered.

'Oh, like what?'

Faith looked her in the eye.

'Like my little sister,' she said. 'She has muscular dystrophy. She's in a wheelchair. We couldn't get the chair through the gate and there was nowhere for her to sit and watch people going by. Now there is.'

Jade felt awful. She hated it when people spoke about her family without thinking, and now she'd done the same.

'I'm sorry,' she said. 'I didn't realize. I was just cross because my mum . . . well, anyway, it was thoughtless of me.'

Faith smiled.

'It's OK,' she said. 'I suppose it's hard for you coming back and finding it all changed. Do you want to come in and look around?'

For a second, Jade was tempted to say yes. She

109

wanted to see her old bedroom. But then she changed her mind. It would almost certainly be different and after all, Tanya was right. It wasn't her home any more. She didn't belong.

'No thanks.' She turned to Tanya. 'Shall we go for a coffee and catch up on the news?'

Her friend shook her head.

'Sorry – can't. Me and Faith are going to this brill new disco that's opened on the pier and I have absolutely zilch to wear. I have to do some serious shopping. Good to see you, Jade.'

Jade felt hollow. She'd always been Tanya's best friend. Now it seemed she had someone new.

'Write, won't you?' Jade called after her. 'And come up to stay?'

But Tanya was already too far down the hill to hear.

3.30 p.m.

'Anyone seen Jade?' Scott wielded his croquet mallet and whacked a ball through one of the hoops.

Tansy shook her head.

'I think she took a bike out,' she said. 'She'll be somewhere on one of the cycle tracks.'

'Cool,' said Scott. 'When I've thrashed you at this, I'll get one and catch her up. I need to talk to her.'

Tansy raised an eyebrow.

'Chat-up time again, is it?' she said teasingly.

'Get lost,' muttered Scott.

3.40 p.m. Warm welcome

As Jade cycled round the corner into Buckingham Street, she realized that before she got to her grand-mother's house she needed a plan. For one thing, she had to hide the bike. Her gran, Charlotte, was great fun but she was a stickler for doing the right thing, and if she found out that Jade had bunked off from a school trip, she would go ballistic. She'd have to tell her that she had come down from Dunchester by train to surprise her. That would explain why she couldn't stay long.

She leaned the bicycle against the side of a bus shelter, smoothed her spiky hair and rang her grand-mother's doorbell.

'Jade! My darling! Oh . . . oh, what a wonderful surprise!'

Jade was enveloped in a bear-like hug and squeezed until she could hardly breathe.

'Oh, Gran, it's so good to see you! I've missed you so much.'

Her grandmother held her at arm's length.

'Look at you!' she said. 'So grown up. Like the haircut.'

Jade blinked.

'You do?' she said.

'Not really,' grinned her grandmother, 'but one doesn't like to seem elderly. One has to be – what do you call it? – trendy.'

Jade grinned.

'You are,' she said. Jade's grandmother had once

been something rather big in the City and still dressed in elegant suits and heeled shoes and went to cocktail parties where, if Dad was to be believed, she got exceedingly talkative on Pimms.

'Now, where are David and Paula? Parking the car?'

She ushered Jade into the narrow hallway.

'They didn't come,' said Jade. 'I came alone.'

Her grandmother looked concerned.

'On the train? On your own? Oh, darling, I don't know that I like – but still, here you are and it's lovely to see you. Let's make some tea and have a good old chat.'

4.00 p.m. Wishing

Andy kicked at an empty coke can and gazed out over the choppy sea. He had been an idiot. Fancy even thinking there was any point looking for his mother in a huge town like this. He had walked from the Peace Memorial all the way along to Palace Pier and back, pushing his bike and scanning the crowds for the tall, elegant shape of his mum. Nothing.

He wondered how Jade was getting on. At least she knew her grandmother would be there; warm and welcoming and safe. He felt a lump come to his throat. At fourteen he shouldn't cry, especially in public. It was OK for Ricky – no one minded if a seven-year-old sobbed his heart out. There were times when Andy thought it must be very nice to be little.

4.15 p.m. Heart to heart

'And so, you see, I really do want to come and live with you.'

Her grandmother picked up the teapot and calmly poured out another cup.

'Darling, that wouldn't do. It wouldn't do at all.'

Jade stared at her.

'What do you mean?' she gasped. 'I wouldn't be any trouble, honestly.'

Charlotte smiled.

'Darling, it's not that. For one thing, you need to be with young people your own age and, for another, I won't be here.'

Jade was aghast.

'What do you mean?' she cried.

Her grandmother took her hand.

'After your father died, I was devastated,' she said. 'That's why I went to stay with Alice in America – to escape the memories, to avoid seeing your house every day.'

Jade nodded.

'I saw it,' she said. 'It looks horrible.'

'Things change,' said her gran calmly. 'Anyway, in the States I had a great time. Oh, don't get me wrong – not a day went by without my thinking of Rob and Lizzie, and missing you – but I had so many new experiences. I even went white-water rafting,' she added smugly.

'At your age!' Jade exclaimed.

'Excuse me,' said her grandmother. 'Seventy-two

may seem ancient to you but I'm not quite ready for the rocking chair and slippers yet.'

Jade laughed despite herself.

'I want to go back,' her gran said. 'Not for good – just for a few months each year. I can't afford to do that and live here, so I'm selling up and taking a one-bedroom flat in Hove. So you see, angel, there would be no room for you anyway.'

Jade looked crestfallen.

'And just think, you've got those lovely friends you wrote to me about – Holly, isn't it? And Cleo?'

Jade nodded.

'Yes, they're cool,' she admitted. 'It's Paula that's the problem. She won't talk about things. I mean, it's as if she's forgotten all about Mum. I thought they were really close.'

'Oh, they were,' agreed her gran. 'Paula really leaned on Lizzie. I think your auntie must be missing your mum terribly.'

'So why won't she talk about it?' persisted Jade.

'Maybe', said her gran, 'she's scared to show how much it hurts. Maybe you have to make her talk.'

Jade nodded thoughtfully.

'I think', said her gran, 'these might help.'

She opened her bureau and took out a brown envelope. It was stuffed full of pictures.

'They were in your mum's cabinet,' she said.

Jade opened the envelope and took out a handful of photographs. There was one of her mum in a Guide uniform with Paula as a very shy-looking

Brownie at her side, and another of Jade as a tiny baby, asleep in Paula's arms.

She touched them with her forefinger.

'Oh, Gran,' she breathed.

'Take them. They're yours. And they might just be what you need.'

4.40 p.m. Waiting on the corner

Andy stood at the corner of Western Road, tapping his foot and eyeing his watch anxiously. Where was Jade? If they didn't get moving soon, they'd be late back and then there really would be trouble.

What a wasted afternoon. He wished he had asked Tansy to come. Then he might not feel quite so alone.

4.45 p.m. Time flies

Three slices of flapjack and a cream bun later, Jade glanced up at the clock. 4.45!

'Gran, I have to go!' she said, leaping to her feet. 'I'll miss the train.'

Her grandmother stood up.

'Come down soon, darling – for a whole weekend. I'll talk to Paula.'

Jade nodded and gave her a hug.

'I do love you, Gran,' she said.

'And I love you too. And remember, never forget the past but don't let it cloud the future. Bye, darling!'

4.48 p.m. Missing property

Jade tore up to the bus shelter and stopped. She looked frantically from left to right.

The bike had gone.

It couldn't have! She slumped against the wall. What now? She couldn't go back to her grandmother and admit the truth. But how would she get back?

Then she remembered Andy, who must be wondering where she was. She could ride back to Downsview on the back of his bike. They wouldn't make it on time but maybe no one would notice.

Sending up a silent prayer that Beetle and Birdie wouldn't be on the ball tonight, and not daring even to contemplate how she would explain a missing bike, she flew down the hill.

4.50 p.m. A face in the crowd

I'll give her five more minutes, thought Andy. And then I'll go. He glanced along the road to see if she was coming.

And that was when he saw her in the distance, pushing her way through the late-afternoon shoppers. Tall and elegant. In the sunflower-patterned dress that Ricky called her happy dress. His mum.

Heart racing, he grabbed his bike, leapt astride and began pedalling along the road. The woman turned to look in a department-store window.

'Mum! Mum!' he cried, his voice choking in his excitement. 'Wait! It's me!'

4.51 p.m.

Jade belted round the corner into Western Road and dashed up to the doorway where she and Andy had agreed to meet.

He wasn't there.

He must have got fed up with waiting and gone without her.

Now she was going to be found out. Not only would she be in trouble for bunking off, but she'd lost a valuable bicycle and you could bet your life the school would make Paula pay and then she'd like Jade even less.

She leaned against the shop window, suddenly feeling alone and scared and stupid. She'd have to go back to Gran's house and tell her the truth. Two tears trickled down her chin.

'My dear, what is it?' A tall woman in a dress covered with orange sunflowers looked down at her. 'Are you in trouble?'

Jade shook her head and sniffed.

'My bike was stolen,' she muttered. 'I'm OK.'

She was about to move away when she saw Andy belting up on his bike. He leapt off, totally ignoring her and grabbed the woman's arm.

'Mum!' he cried.

The woman turned, an astonished expression on her immaculately made-up features.

'Mum, it's . . . oh. Oh. Sorry. I thought you were someone else.'

117

4.53 p.m. Back at base

'I don't understand it,' said Scott, as they queued at the drinks machine. 'I've cycled three times round each track and I can't find her anywhere.'

Holly frowned.

'I didn't see her either,' she said.

'Well,' said Cleo, 'that's hardly surprising since you spent the entire afternoon in pursuit of Paul. You wouldn't have noticed if the queen had nipped out from behind a bush.'

Holly stuck her tongue out.

'I can't find Andy either,' said Tansy, pulling the ring off a can of orange. 'The instructor said he took a bike out – not that he told me.'

Holly grinned.

'Perhaps they are having a secret love affair,' she giggled.

And stopped.

The expressions on Scott and Tansy's faces told her she wasn't being very funny.

4.56 p.m. Trying to help

'I'm sorry,' Jade said for the fifth time. 'I wish it had been your mum.'

Andy shrugged.

'Well, it wasn't, and now you've lost a bike and we're going to be late and the whole day has been a disaster.'

He tightened the strap on his safety helmet.

'I'll just have to climb on the back of your bike and

118

we'll get home that way,' said Jade.

Andy nodded.

'Just pray that no one has noticed we are missing,' he said.

5.00 p.m. Family input

Jade's grandmother decided she could dither no longer. She picked up the telephone and dialled Paula's number.

'Paula? Is that you? Charlotte here, dear. It was so lovely to see Jade today but I honestly don't feel that you should have let her come all this way on her own. You hear such terrible . . . I beg your pardon?'

As she listened to the conversation at the other end of the phone, her mouth fell open and the colour drained from her face.

'But she told me she had a train to catch . . . Oh, my dear . . . Yes, yes, I think you should. Phone the Centre right away. And let me know what happens.'

5.01 p.m. Taking action

'I'm going to tell Miss Partridge,' declared Tansy. 'They might have been attacked, or had an accident and be lying in a ditch somewhere.'

Or Jade might be trying it on with my boyfriend, she thought. In which case we can't move fast enough.

'I think', said Holly, 'we might be saved the bother. Here comes Birdie and she doesn't look happy.'

Miss Partridge strode up to them.

119

'Have any of you seen Andrew Richards or Jade Williams?'

They shook their heads.

'Right,' she said and bustled off again.

'I think', said Holly, 'it's about to be all systems go.'

5.03 p.m. *Pedal power*

'This is harder than I thought,' panted Andy, pulling into the side of the road and wiping the sweat from his brow. 'It's going to take ages.'

'Don't stop,' pleaded Jade. 'We're wasting time.'

They had gone a few hundred metres more when a car overtook them. A police car. It pulled in front of them, and the stop sign on the rear began flashing.

'Oh no,' breathed Andy.

An officer climbed out of the driving seat and walked over to them.

'Do you realize', he said, 'just how dangerous it is to carry a pillion rider on a pedal cycle? And that cycling without a helmet is the height of stupidity, young lady?'

Jade tried to look innocent.

'My bike was stolen,' she said. 'And we have to get back to Downsview before they discover we're missing and . . .'

She stopped as Andy's heel kicked her.

'I see,' said the officer. 'I think the three of us had better have a little chat, don't you?'

5.05 p.m. Red alert

Paula slammed the phone down and put a hand to her forehead. This was all her fault. If she'd let Jade visit her gran as she had begged her to do she would never have run off. She'd have to phone the Centre. And what were they going to think of her? Some rotten substitute parent she had turned out to be.

She was just about to call the Centre when the phone shrilled.

'Yes?' she said abruptly. 'Oh . . . Mr Grubb. Yes, I know. Her grandmother rang. She's gone there.'

The kitchen door opened and Allegra burst in.

'Who's on the phone?' she demanded.

Paula waved a hand and gestured to her to be quiet.

'A bicycle? Oh dear. But anything could happen . . . I see. Well, you will let me know, won't you? The minute you hear anything.'

She put the phone down and began to cry.

'Mum! Mum, whatever is it?'

Paula sniffed.

'It's Jade,' she said. 'She's run away. And it's all my fault.'

5.30 p.m. Reception committee

Miss Partridge and Mr Grubb were standing on the steps when the police car pulled up. There were faces at every window, and under different circumstances Jade might have felt quite important. Right now, she felt very sick and rather small.

'Thank you for phoning us, officer,' said Mr Grubb. 'We'll take over now.'

The policeman nodded.

'I've reported the bike stolen, sir,' he said. 'I'll let you know if we have any news. Not that I hold out much hope.'

Mr Grubb turned to Andy.

'Right, Andrew, come with me. Miss Partridge, I think you have something to say to Jade?'

Jade steeled herself for the ordeal to come.

5.35 p.m. Apologies all round

Miss Partridge led Jade into a small room and shut the door.

'There's the phone,' she said clamly. 'I suggest you ring your aunt. She's frantic with worry.'

'You didn't phone her?' gasped Jade.

'Of course, but she already knew. She'd spoken to your gran.'

I am as good as dead, thought Jade, reluctantly dialling the number. Now she really will hate me.

'Paula? It's me. I'm sorry.'

'Oh, darling, thank goodness you're all right. We've all been so worried. Nell's in tears, Allegra won't eat her supper – thank heavens you rang.'

Jade swallowed.

'I didn't mean to cause trouble. I just wanted to see Gran and to talk about things and –'

'I know, darling. Just come home safely and we'll talk. We'll talk all you want. And Jade?'

'Yes?'

'Please try not to hate me too much.'

Jade bit her lip.

'I don't hate you,' she said. 'Honestly I don't.'

And to her surprise, she realized she meant it.

7.30 p.m. Reunions

When Jade got back to the girls' room, Holly, Tansy and Cleo were rushing around in their underwear getting ready for the disco.

'Jade! You're back! What happened? Did you get a real rollicking? Where did you go?'

They all clamoured for news at the same time.

'Did you go off with Andy?' demanded Tansy.

Jade grinned.

'Not off as in off,' she assured her. 'I wanted to see Gran, he hoped he'd find his mum – oh, can we talk about it all later? I feel a total idiot.'

Cleo smiled.

'Scott will be pleased to see you,' she said. 'He didn't have seconds of anything for supper. And if that isn't a sign of love, I don't know what is.'

For some reason that made Jade feel happier than she had done all day.

8.30 p.m.

An hour later, she discovered she was wrong. She was getting happier by the minute. She was dancing with Scott and they were having a whispered conversation.

'I'm sorry I was such a jerk,' he said. 'Going on and on about wanting you to be happy all the time. Just as long as you still – well, you know.'

'Still what?' urged Jade wickedly.

'Love me,' whispered Scott.

Jade's heart swelled till she thought it would burst through her chest.

'I do,' she whispered back. 'I really do.'

8.45 p.m.

Andy was treading on Tansy's toes with great regularity. Dancing was not his strongest point.

'I should have told you what I was planning to do,' he said. 'You'd have stopped me. You're so sensible.'

Tansy frowned. Sophisticated, hopefully. But sensible? Mega boring.

'I think what you did was really go-getty,' she said. 'And one day we will find your mum.'

'We?' asked Andy with a small smile.

'Yes,' said Tansy very firmly. 'We.'

9.00 p.m. Ego-boosting

'You know,' said Cleo to Trig as they sat on the sidelines sharing a can of ginger beer, 'I would never have had the guts to do what Jade and Andy did. I'm such a wimp.'

Trig shook his head.

'No you're not – why do you always put yourself down?'

Cleo shrugged.

'You had a go at everything even though you were scared – that's being really brave.'

Cleo smiled.

'You're lovely,' said Trig.

And kissed her.

Cleo decided that this was the best activity she had engaged in all weekend.

9.10 p.m.

Paul tapped Holly on the shoulder.

'Dance?' he asked.

Holly nodded in what she hoped was a coolly offhand manner.

'I was wondering', said Paul, 'whether you'd like me to teach you to sail. Properly. On Dunchester Lakes.'

He's asking me out, thought Holly joyfully. We'll be an item. Briefly she pictured herself in a small yacht, her hair blowing in the breeze, Paul staring at her adoringly.

She took a deep breath.

'I really don't think I want to sail.'

Paul looked at her quizzically.

'I was terrified,' she admitted. 'I've had it with trying to be something I'm not.'

Paul looked downcast.

'So you don't want to go out with me?' he said.

'I'd love to,' she laughed. 'As long as you promise it will be on dry land.'

SUNDAY

1.00 p.m. Home again

Paula drove into the school car park and manoeuvred her Metro into the last available space. The coach wasn't due back for another ten minutes but already a cluster of parents was gathering by the gate.

'Excuse me, but are you Jade Williams' guardian?' A tall, thickset man with greying hair and red cheeks approached Paula anxiously.

'Yes, I am,' she replied, puzzled that she didn't recognize the guy.

'I'm Allan Richards,' he said. 'Andy's father. I want to apologize. I think it was my son's fault that Jade was in trouble yesterday.'

Paula smiled and shook her head.

'On the contrary,' she said, 'I gather that it was all Jade's idea. She misses her mother so.'

Allan nodded.

'But at least she has you – I try to be mum and dad

to my boy and get it wrong every time. I'm sorry – I shouldn't be talking like this.'

Paula smiled.

'Oh, please,' she said, 'don't apologize. It's comforting to know I'm not the only one who messes up on a regular basis.

1.05 p.m.

Cleo clambered off the bus, closely followed by Trig and the others.

Her mum was standing by the car, deep in conversation with Holly's mother.

'. . . and so I said to him, you just give me the knickers and leave the rest to me,' Diana was enthusing.

'Indeed?' Angela Vine murmured. 'How fascinating. Oh, look, here are the girls.'

'Darling!' Diana threw open her arms and hugged Cleo. 'Did you have the greatest fun? Was it all too exhausting?'

Cleo cringed. Whenever her mother was in work, she turned all actressy and gushy which was hugely embarrassing, especially since all her friends had normal mothers.

'Mum! Don't!' she hissed.

'Darling, I got the job,' Diana gushed. 'I am so thrilled. I want to tell you all about it.'

Not here you don't, thought Cleo.

'Mum?'

'Yes, treasure?'

'Get in the car. Now.'

1.12 p.m.

Jade had been expecting Paula to totally flip but instead she had given her a quick hug, bundled her into the car and driven off. Halfway home, she turned the car into Beckets Park and turned off the engine.

'Let's walk,' she said.

Here it comes, thought Jade. I might as well get in first.

'Paula, I'm sorry. Really. I know I shouldn't have gone off like that. I was just in such a muddle.'

Paula squeezed her hand.

'What you did was crazy,' she said. 'And we've still to talk about paying for that bicycle. But first, there are more important things to talk about. Like your mum. Like Lizzie.'

Jade gazed at her.

'You do want to talk, don't you?' questioned Paula.

'Oh yes,' said Jade. 'Yes, I do.'

'We'd had a row, you see,' said Paula with a catch in her voice. 'Just three days before the . . . before she died.'

'A row?' Jade was astonished. Her mum and Paula were always all over one another when they met.

Paula nodded.

'She said I was being unfair on Nell,' sighed Paula. 'I'd told her about how I sometimes wished that I hadn't had her, how I wasn't getting any younger . . .'

Jade gasped involuntarily. She remembered the words she had heard behind the closed doors of David's study earlier that week.

'Nell? It was Nell you wished you hadn't had? Not me!'

Paula stared at her.

'You? Of course not, darling. And, of course, I love Nell to bits and pieces too. It's just that she is so shy and timid and whines all the time. She's so unlike Allegra was at the same age, I sometimes don't know how to handle her.'

Jade started thinking.

'Anyway,' Paula continued, 'I shouted at Lizzie and told her that she had it easy, that anyone could cope with one child and she should try having three to deal with. I don't know what made me do it – she always wanted another baby after you but it just didn't happen. I was so horrid to her. And that was the last time we spoke.'

Jade saw that her aunt's eyes were wet with tears.

'Mum would have understood,' she said gently. 'Everyone fights sometimes.'

Paula nodded.

'But Lizzie was always there for me. Always,' she said. 'When our mum died, she took charge of me. When I was bullied at school for being so thin and weedy, she stood up for me. And now she's gone too.'

She paused, and Jade noticed that her shoulders were shaking. Shyly she took her hand.

'Come back to the car,' she said. 'I've got something to show you.'

1.20 p.m.

'Oh, I remember that!' exclaimed Paula with a grin, picking up another photograph. 'Lizzie dressed up as nurse and made me be the patient. Only she stuck the plaster over my mouth because she said I talked too much for a sick person!'

Jade burst out laughing

'And will you look at this!' cried Paula. 'Those platform heels! I thought I was so trendy.'

She turned to Jade.

'You know,' she said, 'I've never taken out my photo albums since the day of the accident. I couldn't face them. Now I think I can. Let's go home.'

'Wait.' Jade lay a hand on her arm. 'About Nell . . .'

'Oh, darling, take no notice. She'll sort herself out.'

Jade shook her head.

'No, she won't,' she declared firmly. 'We have to do that. You and me.'

1.35 p.m.

When they got home, Allegra was standing in the doorway. Jade fully expected snide remarks and comments about how juvenile she was and how much trouble she had caused everyone, so she was very surprised when her cousin grinned and gave her a hug.

'I'll kill you for frightening us all like that!' she said,

but there was a note of teasing in her voice. 'Did you really get arrested?'

'Hardly!' laughed Jade. 'I'll tell you all about it later. Where's Nell?'

1.40 p.m.

'You went away,' said Nell accusingly.

'Well, I'm back now,' said Jade. 'And I've been thinking.'

'What?'

'Well, you haven't told me that some nasty kids at school are bullying you, have you?'

Nell shook her head furiously.

'And you didn't say that they asked you for money, did you?'

More frantic headshaking.

'And you didn't tell me that it was Amanda and Jane and Susie . . .'

Jade tried frantically to think of the names of more of Nell's friends.

'It wasn't them, silly! It was Emily and Rebecca in Year Four.'

She stopped and clamped her hand over her mouth.

'That's it, of course,' said Jade. 'But you didn't tell me that.'

Nell eyed her.

'I didn't tell you that they called me Nellie the Elephant 'cos I'm fat and horrible, did I?'

Jade shook her head. How could anyone be so horrid?

'They'll cut off my hair if you tell,' she said. 'Then I'll look all funny like you.'

Jade laughed.

'Oh, Nell,' she said, 'I do love you.'

'I love you too,' said Nell. 'Will it all come right?'

Jade hugged her.

'It will,' she said, 'I promise. And from now on, I shall call you by your real name. And so must you. That will shut them up.'

Nell looked impressed.

'Helen Veronica Madeleine Webb,' she said.

'Helen will do just fine,' laughed Jade. 'Have you ever heard of an elephant called Helen?'

1.50 p.m.

Paula and David sat side by side on the sofa.

'How could we have been so blind?' said David for the third time. 'All that asking for money and crying at night – we should have guessed.'

'I should have known,' said Paula. 'After all, I was teased at school and it was Lizzie who put a stop to it. Yet I couldn't see it in my own child. It took Jade to make us see what was happening under our noses.'

'Thank heavens for you, Jade,' said David. 'I was all set to be mad at you for running off like that but I don't seem to have the energy now! It's just good to have you back.'

Jade grinned.

'It's nice to be back,' she said.

Allegra looked up from the floor where she was building a Lego castle with her sister.

'Oh, please,' she said. 'Can we finish with all this sentimental twaddle and have something to eat? I've got some serious flirting to attend to this evening.'

2.10 p.m.

They were demolishing cheese pie when the phone rang.

'Hi, Jade, it's me – Cleo. Is everything OK?'

'Fine,' said Jade. 'What about you?'

'Don't ask,' said Cleo. 'Portia is locked in the bathroom because Gareth dumped her, Lettie's howling because the goldfish died, and to cap it all my mother is due to appear on national TV in her underwear.'

Jade burst out laughing.

'Well,' she said, 'look on the bright side. It's better than appearing without her underwear.'

'Honestly,' said Cleo, 'they're all manic. Families! Who'd have them? Oh, sorry, Jade, I forgot you haven't got one.'

Jade glanced at the table. Josh was reading *Insect Weekly* and telling his father that he simply had to acquire a pet scorpion, Allegra was picking bits of onion out of her pie and telling her mother that she had put them there purely to give her bad breath for Hugo, and Helen was spelling out her new name in French fries.

'Yes, I have,' she said. 'I have a perfectly manic one of my own.'

Want to find out
what happens to
the girls in
another great
What a Week story?

Then sneak a peek
over the page ...

'Er, Mum,' said Holly, 'you're not going to actually be *at* my party on Saturday, are you? I mean, while it's actually going on?'

Her mother walked purposefully to the fridge and took out a packet of sausages. She was not a mother who worried about low-fat diets.

'No, Holly dear, I am not,' she said, peeling off the cling film.

Thank heavens for that, thought Holly.

'Because I'm afraid you've got a little carried away with all this,' she continued, piercing the sausages with a skewer. 'There is absolutely no way you can have a party on Saturday night.'

Holly's stomach suddenly felt as if it had been filled with lead. No party? There had to be a party. She had told everyone there was going to be a party. Even Dad had agreed that there was going to be a party. What was her mother going on about?

'But, Mum, Saturday's my birthday,' she protested.

'Oh, I know that, darling, of course I do,' chirruped her mother (who in truth had got confused and only remembered when she perused Holly's list in a boring bit of the committee meeting that morning). 'And of course you'll have your presents and I thought maybe a nice cake and then on Sunday you, me and Dad could go to Bella Pasta for lunch . . .'

That did it. No way, thought Holly, am I settling for a slice of chocolate sponge and a dollop of tagliatelle for my fourteenth birthday.

'Mum! I'm not a kid any more – I don't want to celebrate my birthday with my *parents*, for heaven's sake! Get real!'

Her mother raised an eyebrow, which should have been a warning to Holly. She, however, was too irate to notice.

'And anyway, you can't do this to me because Dad said I could have a party!' she shouted. 'What's more, he said I could invite loads of friends – he PROMISED!'

Her mother raised the other eyebrow.

'Oh, he did, did he?' she said.

'Yes he did,' said Holly. 'He said it was a big day and he was looking forward to it.'

Her mother sighed.

'Well, you know your father; he lives in a world of his own. I think you will find you were talking at cross-purposes. Saturday is Dunchester Battle Day. Dad seems to think you are bringing a crowd of mates along to that.'

Dunchester had been the scene of a minor skirmish during the Civil War, when a crowd of hot-headed peasants had taken a stand against a section of Cromwell's army and lost in a rather messy manner involving bodies in the blood-drenched river and limbs lying around in fields. Not content with erecting a plaque in the local church and a statue of a rather distressed-looking farmhand on the river bank, the town had in recent years turned the whole fiasco into a money-making event, with re-enactments of the battle (orchestrated, needless to say, by Holly's father), side shows and a raft race on the River Cress.

Holly's heart sank. Her father surely couldn't have been so thick as to imagine she'd want to take her friends to that naff do.

'So what's that got to do with anything?' demanded Holly, deciding that her mother was just fishing for an excuse not to have to fork out for the food and drink. 'Just because Dad's going to spend the day playing soldiers doesn't mean I can't have a party.'

Her mother sighed.

'Holly, don't you ever take an interest in anything that goes on?' she sighed. 'I do so try to make you aware of social issues.'

And I do try to make you aware of the mess that is my life, thought Holly.

From *What a Week to Fall in Love* – available now!

What a Week to Fall in Love

by Rosie Rushton

Holly's having a *proper* party for her fourteenth birthday – a party that her parents aren't invited to, but boys *definitely* are. Especially Scott, Holly's ex, who she intends to get back from the claws of Ella.

But when her mum cancels the party, Holly devises an extremely clever plan. Unfortunately, clever plans have a way of backfiring, especially where parents are concerned . . .

What a Week
to Make it Big

by Rosie Rushton

There's huge excitement when the girls find out
that a cable-TV quiz show is coming to their
school. This is their big chance to be on TV and
get a taste of fame – as well as meet the *very*
gorgeous presenter.

But not everyone can make it big. Being left out
and suffering from an attack of the green-eyed
monster is no fun at all. It's at times like this
than you find out who your *real* friends are . . .